HOLIDAY ESCAPE

BROTHERHOOD PROTECTORS WORLD

PAM MANTOVANI

BROTHERHOOD PROTECTORS

ORIGINAL SERIES BY ELLE JAMES

for Dale and Tina
who know
age means nothing
to the heart

CHAPTER 1

FOR THE FIRST time in twenty-six years, Samantha Ethridge was back in Los Angeles. She stood outside the studio set, ignoring all the Christmas decorations that contrasted with the warm sunshine, and considered how far she'd traveled. When she'd left LA at eighteen, she'd been full of determination, energy and the hope to make up for a night when she'd run away rather than stand her ground and defend.

In the years since she left, she'd learned ways to defend – herself and countless dignitaries with the Secret Service. She'd been trained to escape – for safety rather than in fear. She still preferred simplicity in her clothing, but now the choice was for expediency rather than economics. She'd traveled the world, met fascinating people, had seen and experienced as much good as not in various cultures.

Meeting Hank Patterson at the consulate in Beirut years earlier had morphed into friendship. When he'd heard of her resignation, he'd contacted her, convinced her to move to Montana and become an integral part of his Brotherhood Protectors elite bodyguard team. She liked the quiet of the countryside, her small cabin, and the freedom to choose her assignments.

The pleasure of that friendship, and the one she'd developed with his wife, along with her expertise as a Secret Service Agent had convinced her to accept this assignment. Of course, she'd assumed she'd only be advising Sadie for this movie. Her mistake had been confirmed once they arrived on set and she was told the sexy leading man would be playing the role of the government agent. She'd been named technical advisor for the entire crew, including him. Her instant attraction to the younger man unsettled her in ways she'd never imagined.

"What do you think?"

Sam turned to face the woman clad in a stunning red evening gown. Diamonds, at least a remarkable facsimile, spread over the cleavage exposed by the gown's neckline. Fulfilling her role as technical advisor, her gaze trailed down, over the snug fit on slim hips, along the slit that went from thigh to hem to reveal mile-high heels that no agent she knew would wear while working an assignment. But every woman watching the movie would covet.

"I can promise you I never had a reason to dress like this when I was in the Service, and no way would I have looked as good as you do."

"I bet you'd look sexy as hell in that dress."

Sam's lips flattened as she turned to the new arrival. Christopher Reardon, in a tuxedo, offered a red rose. The fact that the flower was silk, and a movie prop, added to the illusion of his ridiculous compliment. She blamed the little kick in her pulse on annoyance.

Not the first time he'd frustrated her since they'd met. And not the first time he'd flirted with her. She supposed he expected her to be flattered. After all, he was almost thirteen years her junior. And, yes, older or not, she was female enough to admit he was sinfully attractive.

Samantha admired the dark blonde hair, cut short to fit his role, the eyes that reminded her of the turquoise waters of Aruba, the six-foot height that would put her right under his chin if they stood close. His shoulders were certainly wide enough for a woman to rest her head on and his arms muscular enough to cradle her. With more effort than she was comfortable admitting, she avoided looking at his mouth. She absolutely refused to dwell about what that mouth could do to a woman.

More importantly was the way he talked to her when he started a conversation that had nothing to do with the movie production or any information relating to his character. Naturally, there had been questions and discussions about her job, her advice on how he should play the role. His genuine interest in her viewpoints on the cultures and economies of some of the countries where she'd lived flattered her more than his flirting. During those talks he revealed an interest beyond the superficial, a desire to understand and, to her shame, an empathy she had not expected of him. He'd gone on to speak about a couple of service projects he had in mind to pursue once filming completed.

Still, he was a rising star, the leading man in this drama. She was a retired Secret Service agent. He'd grown up, so she'd read as part of her preparation for the assignment, in a loving family. She'd lived with a single father who worked nights and slept during the day, leaving her alone more often than not. Christopher obviously sought the spotlight. She worked behind the scenes. Their lives could not be more opposite.

"Rehearsing your lines, Mr. Reardon?" Sam asked, ignoring the twinkle of delight in Sadie's gaze.

"That's no line, Sam."

Ordinarily having someone address her with the masculine version of her name never bothered her. Only, when it rolled off Christopher's tongue, it sounded feminine and intimate.

"It hardly matters."

"Oh, it matters." When someone called for him, he glanced over his shoulder and gave a quick nod. "But there's plenty of time yet to convince you."

"Girl," Sadie sighed as both women watched him walk away. "In case you haven't noticed, that man has the hots for you."

"He's young enough to be my . . . brother."

"He doesn't look at you like he thinks of you as a sister." She gave Sam a little elbow nudge. "And you're too trained an observer to pretend otherwise."

"All right." As she could do with few, Sam relaxed and smiled at Sadie. "My keen powers of observation confirm he doesn't look at me like an older sister. That doesn't mean," she hurried on when Sadie opened her mouth. "I'm going to do anything more than observe him in return."

Two hours later, after observing and advising, she admitted it was time for action.

"Let me show you what I have in mind." She looked at the director, got a nod.

The scene they'd been rehearsing, blocking, was one in which the lead characters, Sadie and Christopher, were locked together on a dance floor at a charity function. As the agent with a personal reason for wanting to arrest an international jewel thief, Christopher's character struggled between ethics and love.

If he arrested the woman Sadie played, wearing a necklace made from the loose diamonds of her latest heist, he'd lose the woman he loved. If he let her escape, he'd not only lose her in another way, he'd also lose his principles and self-respect.

Moving into position, Christopher held Sam close, one hand pressed at the small of her back, the other holding hers with a hand harder and more calloused than she'd expected. She knew his body was hard, knew because she'd seen most of it during one memorable scene of the movie where he'd acted in a love scene with Sadie. Now, his blue gaze locked on hers so that, in character, he lowered his mouth to within an inch of hers as he whispered his lines.

"Don't do this. Trust me and I'll find a way to help you."

"No one can help me," she replied, with little to none of the character's remorse. "I started this journey long ago, back when I believed there would never be anything good in my life." Sam swallowed, mentally shook off the character, dismissed the troubling sensation that the dialogue had been much too realistic.

"Now, here, is where I believe Sadie lifts her hand to his cheek." She looked to the director, away from Christopher, for affirmation.

"This is where the man acting as Sadie's accomplice creates a disturbance to allow her to escape?" she asked.

"Yes. When Christopher turns in that direction, Sadie slips away," confirmed the director.

"What if he doesn't turn away?" Sam turned

back to look at Christopher, his hand instinctively closing tighter around hers. "He's an agent, he wouldn't turn loose."

"He'd choose his job over his heart?" Christopher asked.

"Love demands the hardest choices." Her heart drumming, she tore her gaze away from Christopher. "But being a very smart man, he has another plan." She smiled and stepped away from him, looking back at the director to see he was already waving for the screenwriter to join the discussion. It wasn't an inventive plot twist, but she thought it could work, believed the actors could make it plausible. "I'm sorry, but yes, it would be a different ending than the one you had planned."

"You know a way they can work together," Christopher said. "A way they can be together without him compromising his career."

"Well, much depends on what your writers do with what I suggest. And if your director is willing to allow the break in shooting to change the script." She looked over at Sadie. "It will also require re-doing some pivotal scenes."

Despite the extra work involved, Sam found herself sitting in a conference room crowded with the director, writers and the main actors detailing how her plan would play out on screen. At a break, she walked over to the table where coffee had been set out.

"So, did this idea of yours come from personal experience?" Christopher asked.

She glanced at him, then to put a little subtle difference between them, reached for the container at the end of the table holding cream. "My assignments were focused on protection, not apprehension."

"Do I make you nervous, Sam?"

"Of course not," she answered, quickly enough even she heard the thread of unease in her voice. "Why would you think that?"

His mouth curved. "You usually drink your coffee black."

"Look, Christopher." She turned to face him. After all, she'd faced gunfire before, surely she could handle a smug, good-looking actor. Especially one younger than her. Between rehearsal and this meeting cast members had changed out of costumes and into street clothes. Christopher wore faded jeans, a navy buttoned shirt and ragged tennis shoes with the same casual elegance as he'd worn the tuxedo.

"I'm flattered that you would flirt with me. But

I'm here to do a job, not indulge in a movie set romance with someone who'll forget me before he rolls out of bed."

He shot his hand out to stop her from walking away. His eyes were turbulent now, like a sea tossed by a storm. "I'm fascinated, not flirting," he said quietly. "And you haven't answered my question."

"No," she said. "My past has nothing to do with my suggestion for this movie."

"Good." He nodded. "Then there's no ghost I have to worry about slipping into bed with us once we get there."

She tilted her head as if studying him, as if her mind hadn't filled with impossibly vivid erotic images. "I guess that kind of wild imagination is a benefit in your job."

He didn't act annoyed by her quip. Instead he grinned with delight. "No wonder you fascinate me." He leaned in close and it took all of her training to hold still. "Have dinner with me tonight."

"No."

"I'm going to ask again."

"The answer will be the same."

"That's very similar to how this director

answered when I first approached him about wanting this role." She felt a squeeze, glanced down, stunned to see her hand tucked within his. "I'll ask again."

Before she could comment, he turned and walked away.

CHRIS DIDN'T LOOK BACK, although, God knew, he wanted to. He enjoyed putting that stunned look on Sam's face when she realized he'd taken her hand. It made him think of what he'd see once he got her into bed and touched her the way he itched to do.

He couldn't name a single woman that had ever caught his attention and focus the way the sexy former Secret Service agent did. It was more than her looks, although they were stellar. He liked her long, lean lines, the way the top of her head would have tucked right under his chin if he'd been able to hold her close during a real dance rather than the one on set. She wore her reddish-brown hair pulled back in a low ponytail that he figured she used because it required little effort, especially when she was working. What it did for him was expose her ears, and the simple gold studs she wore. He had a serious fantasy playing on a loop in his mind about nibbling right there. Her brown eyes were direct, and a man knew she'd look at him with that same fierce intensity in bed. He knew she was older, only because he'd taken the time to do some research, but he didn't see age lines when he looked at her. He saw the timeless marriage of intelligence, grace, and sensuality.

"Let me help," he said, hurrying over to assist a couple of guys moving furniture for the new set-up.

"Don't let the brass catch you," one of the guys said. "They'll be all in my face for letting their big-time movie star take a chance of getting hurt."

The guy looked to be close to sixty. Curious, and always interested, Christopher asked, "What's the biggest movie you've worked on?"

"I worked on Natalie Roberts first movie."

"Lawless?" Christopher grunted. "That movie stunk."

"Yes, but Natalie Roberts shinned."

"It's the role that made her a star."

"She was a nice person. Still is."

He'd grown up, in a manner of speaking, in the world of movies and stars. As head of accounting at one of the major studios, his father had often brought him along to work. Chris hadn't been interested in accounting or business meetings, but seeing the illusions, watching the action and drama, that had filled his heart and mind. When one of those visits resulted in him securing a part in a successful commercial, he believed he'd taken the first step on his career path. His mother, however, had insisted he have as normal a childhood as possible. So, he'd gone to school, skipping the occasional class, snuck a drink, or two, beneath the bleachers at football games, had some memorable experiences in the back seat of his older brother's car and gone to prom. He'd tried out for every role in every high school drama production, starred in two, and pitched in whenever needed on any of the work that went on behind the curtain.

Waiting to pursue a full-time acting career, and again while waiting for good roles, had taught him patience. A handy trait to possess no matter the vocation. Or, he sat back at the table and watched Sam walk across the room, when you're a man intent on seducing a strong-willed woman.

Unfortunately look was all he'd been able to do. When the meeting ended, his co-star Tyler Collins stopped him from following Samantha.

"Chris, do you think you could come by my trailer in an hour or so and help with some lines?"

The request surprised Christopher. Tyler had never been subtle about stating he should have landed the lead role and claiming Christopher only got the role after a go-round on the casting couch. Too often that kind of comment and antagonism evolved into shouting matches that barely, just barely, ended before the two could come to blows.

"I've got plans for tonight."

"I get it." Tyler followed his gaze to where Samantha was walking away. "An actor of your poor quality is more interested in a piece . . ."

Christopher erupted, pressing his forearm against Tyler's throat as he slammed him against the wall. The room grew quiet. "Watch your mouth," he growled.

"Just calling it the way I see it."

From the corner of his eye, Christopher noticed Samantha watching the incident. As did the remaining cast and crew, all of whom had seen something like this happen between the two men at one time or another. "Fine." He shoved off. "I'll be at your trailer in an hour."

He went to his trailer, drowned his temper in a long shower, helped along by the image of running soapy hands over Samantha, followed by finishing off half a sub sandwich and a cold beer. Gathering up the script, he spotted a messenger bag he didn't recognize peeking out from under the cushioned seat. Recalling it was to be used in the scene he was to rehearse, he tossed it over his shoulder and headed out for Tyler's trailer.

Knocks on the door went unopened, calls to Tyler's cell went unanswered. Irritated, swearing, he started back to his trailer. An unexpected noise, sounding like a punch landing in a soft belly, stopped him before he reached the edge of what had been designed to look like a deserted alley.

"Stop," came a low voice. Christopher looked around a minute before realizing the command had come from deep within the alley. He took a step forward, his eyes beginning to adjust to the darkness. He heard the distinct sound of a moan.

"You said you had it under control." The voice sounded vaguely familiar to Christopher.

"I hid it with Chris until I had time to get it."

"I'm losing patience, Tyler." Christopher went shocked still. "Where is it?"

"It wasn't in his trailer. I don't know what he did with it."

A long windy sigh echoed down the alley.

"Then you're no good to me. I should have known better to trust you with a take this big and important. I had a good thing going here, now you've put a snag in everything. You should have stayed away from the track, Tyler. Take care of him."

"Sure thing," said a new voice.

Christopher heard another blow landing, followed by a long moan and a soft cry of protest. Of begging for the beating to stop.

He peeked around a corner of the building in time to see a man drag a bloodied Tyler to his feet. His eyes widened and he cried out when the man punched him in the stomach.

"Damn it, why did you do that here and now?"

Christopher froze. He now identified the voice, but never had he heard the kind of disgust and dismissal he heard now. He wanted to shake his head, dismiss the suspicion rising in his throat like bile, but knew better than to make a move that would alert the two men to his presence.

He needed time to reconcile the fact that the on-set property manager, Jerry Bellham, had stood by, sounding annoyed, while he directed someone to beat the crap out of Tyler Collins. He drew his cell phone out to call the emergency number with trembling hands.

The man holding up Tyler let him slide to the ground. That's when Christopher realized the man hadn't simply beaten his co-star. He'd stabbed him with a knife. "I can't help it if he stumbled and fell onto the knife."

"Sometimes I wonder why I keep you around," Jerry said.

The man jerked the knife out, wiped it clean with a handkerchief he pulled from his back pocket. "This is why." He grinned and kicked Tyler with his shoe. "You've got cops on the take who'll help cover this up."

Christopher stopped with his thumb on the send button, panic like ice in his veins. What the hell could he do now?

"God knows I pay them enough. Still, let's get out of here before someone comes by and sees us. I've got to find Reardon."

Christopher darted back, pressing his back against the wall as the two men stopped in the doorway. Stunned, holding his breath against the threat of being heard, he stared at the man giving directions. Jerry was a long-time, well-respected fixture in the movie industry. Everyone in the business knew if they needed a specific prop for their sets, there was no one better than Jerry at finding it for you.

In the past six weeks Christopher had worked with this man, had complimented him on the photos of his family, including a new granddaughter, Jerry had proudly showed to anyone who stopped long enough to look. One evening they'd sat opposite each other over a poker game, trying to out-bluff one another. Now Christopher watched as he calmly walked away from a beating and stabbing.

He waited thirty long seconds before he darted inside the building. "Tyler." Kneeling down, he took in the blood, the chest barely lifting with each shallow breath. Trying to avoid the blood, he placed a hand on a shoulder. "Hang on, I'll get help."

Tyler somehow found the strength to lift a hand, close it around the strap of the bag Christopher wore crossed over his chest. "Sorry."

"What the hell's going on?"

"Get away." Blood bubbled on his lips. "He'll find you." His arm dropped to the ground.

For several long seconds he stared in stunned silence, his mind reeling with everything that he'd seen and heard. When he finally rose to his feet and turned, he came face-to-face with Tyler's killer.

"I thought I heard someone when we walked out." He pulled out his knife. "I always trust my instincts." He then pulled out his cell phone, and, keeping his gaze locked with Christopher's, punched a button. "I found your boy," he said into the phone. His grin had a greasy ball of nerves rolling in Christopher's stomach. "I'll do that." With another punch, he disconnected the call. "Now, you and I are going to have a little talk."

It wasn't a conscious decision. Christopher simply acted. Using a move he remembered Sam telling him about, he rose on the balls of his feet, waited. When the man was within arm's length, he shot forward, his shoulder lowered so it could plow into the man's stomach. The force and unanticipated move enable him to shove the man aside. There was a burn along his arm but he didn't stop or slow. One clear thought cut through everything.

Run.

CHAPTER 2

SAMANTHA CLOSED the trailer door behind her, stepping outside to give Sadie some privacy for the phone call with her husband. She'd made the mistake the first night of filming of staying inside and overhearing some tantalizing bits of conversation between husband and wife. Still, it was nice to hear a marriage thriving through years, children and the distance that sometime separated them.

What would it be like to share her world with someone? To accept their faults along with their strengths? To take an interest in their life and know they did the same with yours? The longing that struck hard and strong took her by surprise. Until she'd met someone during the last months of her last assignment, she'd always kept her interactions casual, temporary. Only to watch him turn from her and reach for another woman. She'd lost more than the chance for love that day, she lost a little bit of self-respect.

With her Secret Service career behind her and building her reputation with the Brotherhood Protectors, not to mention adjusting to living in one place full time, she'd regained her confidence. But she hadn't had the interest, or taken the time, to consider if she wanted more.

Only now, despite her efforts, her mind traveled to Christopher. Her initial impression, based on gossip and rumor, had been he was simply the latest in a long string of young actors that believed everyone and everything revolved around him and his desires. Instead she discovered a hard-working, well-liked and idealistic young man.

He tempted her to ignore the age difference between them and enjoy having him in her bed for as long as it lasted. If she'd read him right, and she had, she knew he wanted her. And she thought, ruefully, she was probably the only woman alive, of any age, who would hesitate taking him up on his unspoken offer.

Not that she hadn't had her share of short-term affairs. In fact, she had once been with a man two years younger. The age difference between her and Christopher might be greater than those two years, but neither one of them expected anything more than to enjoy one another for the short term. Still, it would be her decision, her choice, whether or not to explore this fascinating interest.

"Sam."

She spun around, more than a little chagrinned that she'd been so deep in thought that she hadn't heard him approach. Her gaze narrowed. He stood in the shadow of the trailer but as she watched he swayed a little. "What's wrong?" she asked. "Have you been drinking?" She stepped forward, stopping short when he came into view in a thin slice of light from the trailer window. "Oh, God," she whispered, going to him, reaching for his arm. "Is that blood? Are you hurt?"

Before he could answer, she heard a noise. Christopher pushed her back further into the shadows and lifted a hand to cover her mouth, surprising her.

Putting his mouth to her ear, he whispered, "Quiet."

With a nod she indicated she understood. Looking over his shoulder she watched as a man, someone she recognized from the movie set, knocked on Sadie's door. She felt Christopher stiffen. With a subtle press of her body, she had him backing off enough that she could reach for the gun holstered at the small of her back. The man drew in a deep breath, knocked on the door again.

"Hey, Jerry," Sadie said when she opened the door.

"Ms. Sadie." He pulled a handkerchief out of his back pocket and swiped it over his eyes. "Have you seen Christopher?"

"No." She gestured with the phone in her hand. "I've been talking with my husband. What's wrong? You look upset."

"It's Tyler, he's dead."

"What?"

"I found him over on sound stage three. I know he and Christopher were going to rehearse."

"You can't think Christopher would do this."

"I wouldn't have thought so until earlier today, when they nearly went to blows over that woman."

Sadie straightened her shoulders. "That woman is my friend, and you can't convince me either one of them would do what you're saying happened. Just a minute," she said before lifting the phone to her ear. "Hold on, Hank. Let me find out what's going on."

"No, you stay here," Jerry said, backing away from the door, stopping her from stepping outside. "Just don't open your door if Christopher comes by." He turned and hurried away.

Sam stood her ground for another thirty seconds before she released the grip on her gun.

"What's going on?" she whispered.

"He killed Tyler," Christopher answered, keeping his voice low. "I mean." He swiped a hand over his eyes and she could make out the shocked expression of someone who'd witnessed death. "The man with him did. And they're going to blame me. Jerry pays off cops, he bragged about it. They'll believe him." He tilted his head toward the trailer. "That's why he went to Sadie's trailer. To make sure everyone remembers the fight today."

"What happened?"

"Tyler didn't show for the rehearsal he said he wanted. I cut through the lot." He managed a small smile. "I was thinking of coming here and talking you into a late dinner."

"You mean into your bed."

"I hoped." His lips flattened. "I heard arguing. Tyler was on the ground. He'd been beaten. He was moaning, crying, telling Jerry it wasn't where it should have been."

"What wasn't?"

He drew in a breath. "I don't know, he died before he could tell me." He explained how he used the move she'd told him about to evade the man before running over here. "You heard Jerry. He's going to tell everyone that I killed Tyler. I swear to you." He met her gaze and she could see the fear glittering in his eyes. "I didn't kill him."

"Of course, you didn't."

Sam looked over at the trailer, considering how best to proceed. She didn't want to leave without telling Sadie what had happened, but she didn't want to risk her friend becoming involved and possibly hurt.

"Shit," Christopher said when his cell phone rang. He pulled it out of his back pocket, looked at the screen. "It's Jerry."

Sam grabbed it from him, threw it onto the ground, and used the heel of her shoe to demolish the device. That's when she caught another, just as deadly sound. The increasing volume of sirens.

"What do we do now?" Christopher asked.

"We run."

Grabbing his hand, she led them between a row

of trailers. "No," Christopher said when she turned to the right. "That leads back to Tyler's. This way." He pointed straight ahead. It meant crossing an empty lot, but she trusted him. With him now in the lead, they ran as fast as they could, bent over, hoping to minimize their visibility.

She lost count of how many alleys, real and false, they darted down or raced by. Same with storefronts. It wasn't her style to rush without taking time to check, and re-check as needed, before proceeding, but the situation demanded speed. Christopher moved as if he owned the property, certainly as if he had the layout printed in his mind. While she'd admired his build, she learned first-hand it wasn't all for show. He never tired, kept a steady hand around hers, and once lifted her over a chain-link fence. Finally, they made their way off studio grounds by squeezing between the locked gates of an abandoned back entrance.

"Now what?" he asked.

She looked up and down the street. "We need to find a car. Then, I have to make a call."

A couple of hours later, as they sat in the non-descript sedan where a lazy driver had left the remote starting fob tucked inside the console, Sam ended the phone call with Hank Patterson.

"Why aren't you destroying your cell phone?"

"No one's looking for me. At least not yet," she said. "Where's the nearest ATM machine?"

Following Christopher's directions, she got as much of a cash advance on her credit card as possible. If she was tracked, the authorities would have no trouble discovering she'd withdrawn the funds. Until they did, if they did, she'd take whatever actions were needed to keep Christopher safe. With the help of the car's navigation system, they stopped at a discount store.

"I'm not staying in the car," he argued when she made the suggestion.

"Look, if you go inside, we run the risk of someone recognizing you."

"I'm not that famous." He paused. "Yet."

His fame wasn't the only thing that concerned her. He didn't have to be famous to capture attention. His looks, hell the entire package, were way too eye-catching. No one who saw his body, that head of hair begging for a woman's hands, or those eyes that were direct and interested when you talked, would ever forget meeting him.

"I didn't go to all this trouble to get into more at the first step," she said.

"Technically, this is the second. The first was withdrawing money."

"This isn't a scene from one of your movies, Christopher. It's real life."

As soon as the words were out, she regretted them.

"You think I don't know that?" he asked, his voice low and filled with torment. "You think I'm ever going to forget looking into the face of a man while he dies?" He shook his head, looked out the side window.

Wanting, perhaps needing, to make amends, she touched a hand to his arm. She knew how often lifeless eyes could haunt a person's thoughts or sleep. "I'm sorry, that was callous of me."

They sat in silence a little longer. Finally, he opened his door and got out, circling around the hood to open her door. With a smile as false as the happy tone in his voice, he held out his hand. "Ready, sweetheart?"

She shut down the engine and stepped out, pocketing the fob as a way to avoid his offered hand. "Oh, come on now, don't be mad." He hurried after her, caught her arm and pulled her close so he could whisper in her ear, "Trust me, people will remember a couple fighting. They'll turn away from one that doesn't do anything more interesting than hold on to each other as they walk."

He was right, she knew that. Few people paid attention to happy couples. It also reminded her that he earned his living by acting. Even so, she enjoyed the feel of his warm body against hers, the weight of his arm around her.

Going with the scene he set up, she turned her head and nipped his ear lobe. "Trust me, sugar," she said, layering on a southern accent. "You'll know when I'm mad."

He chuckled. "I have no doubt."

Arm-in-arm they walked into the store. By unspoken agreement they kept to simple jeans, T-shirts and underwear, followed by a few basic toiletries. She didn't notice he'd added a box of condoms until they were at check-out. She refused to make any comment. But, God, her thoughts were loud and clear. And more erotic than anything she'd ever experienced.

As they walked out, Christopher paused beside the charity bucket, dug some bills out of his pocket, and stuffed them with a cheery "Merry

Christmas" for the bell-ringer. It was impossible not to be warmed by his generosity. She just hoped there didn't come a time when that cash would come in handy.

It was ridiculous, she decided while cranking the engine to life. They were pretty much on the run from the cops, at least until a couple of Brotherhood Protectors unearthed some information to clear up this situation, and she struggled to keep her hands and mouth off an attractive, younger, man.

They picked up some food at a fast-food drive-thru, eating while they rode around, appearing to be nothing more than a couple out for a drive to admire the Christmas lights and decorations. Twice they were passed by a cop car but Sam kept pace with the traffic around her. Finally, they made their way out of the city limits, rolling to a stop at the kind of roadside motel that took cash and asked no questions.

Christopher didn't argue this time when she mentioned him staying in the car while she paid for the room. She didn't question his sudden acquiescence. She knew how adrenaline could keep you running for only so long before it drained away, leaving you subdued and pensive.

They each grabbed a share of the assorted bags and entered the small room.

Sam swore. She'd focused only on handing over the cash and getting away before the clerk took too close a look. She hadn't thought to ask for two beds. Christopher crossed the room to toss down the shopping bags, along with the messenger bag she'd all but forgotten he'd been holding onto this entire time.

He turned on the television and found a news channel. Not surprisingly, Tyler's death was the lead story. They sat side-by-side on the end of the bed and stared at the screen as the camera zoomed in on Jerry Bellham's face.

"I never would've guessed. Christopher was a nice guy. Sure, him and Tyler had words sometimes but. . . " He trailed off, shaking his head.

"And you have no idea how he managed to swap the movie necklace with real diamonds?"

"None. I'm sick about it. I mean, that's my department and for him to do something like this, right under my nose. I thought he was really interested in me and what I do." He again shook his head. "To learn he used me and my job hurts."

"That son of a bitch." Christopher shot to his feet. "No way." He spun around, stared down at

Sam. "I swear to you, I have nothing to do with stolen diamonds."

Sam sat on the edge of the bed and studied him. He stood braced, legs apart, hands fisted at his sides, as if preparing to do battle. She supposed that was an accurate enough analogy. Anger, not fear, showed through the fierce look in his eyes, in the firm line of his mouth.

"Christopher, sit down."

Before he could another voice had him spinning back to stare at the television. Sam didn't need the identification insert at the bottom of the screen to tell her this was Christopher's mother. He had her eyes, and although hers were tearfilled, they shared the same desperate look. Next to her a tall man with Christopher's hair, his father, supported her with an arm around her shoulder.

"No way would my son do what he's been accused of. I'm telling you you're wrong. Find him and you'll see I'm right. Find him so I can know he's not hurt. Find him," she repeated, breaking down, the tears falling as she turned into her husband's arms.

The screen now showed a picture of him, one she assumed was a studio publicity shot, as the reporter droned on about him being the proverbial person of interest. There was more, she heard some speculation about the diamonds, but all she saw and heard was Christopher.

"I've got to call her." He stood, patted his pockets. "Damn it, you killed my phone. Where's yours?" He grabbed the bags of their earlier purchases off the bed and flung them against the wall. His messenger bag went flying next.

"Christopher." She gripped his arms, held him still. "You can't."

"Don't tell me I can't call her." As much as her hold allowed, he flung out a hand, pointing at the television. "Did you see her? She thinks I'm dead."

Sam stared into his eyes, saw the storm of frustration and, more, the love for his family. Seeing his mother's distress had broken his control on his emotions. The familial connection, love and faith, released the frustration and fear he'd buried to this point. She didn't know how to comfort him, didn't know any words that would relieve worry or make the situation better. Giving someone something you'd never received yourself was hard. A distant part of her, a part that died years earlier on a warm LA night, rose up to clog her throat.

She usually focused solely on the physical, on the logic and steps necessary to protect. This search for a way to offer emotional comfort opened her to a risk far more dangerous than any she'd ever faced before.

As she stared into his eyes, as she felt the flex of the muscles she held, another sensation crept between them. One more primitive and private than the drama playing out on every news station in the city. Seductive, so intense, that for a long moment all she could do was wait. And want. She watched his gaze drop to her mouth, saw the intent darken the blue of his eyes. It crossed her mind that this was one way to temper his outburst, to relieve his worry and take his mind off a call that couldn't be made.

"You can't," she whispered when he began to lower his mouth to hers. She'd never regretted anything more in her life than this refusal.

He studied her a little longer. Then, with a long sigh, he stepped back. The temper may have faded but the worry flooded back into his eyes as he glanced away. She didn't entirely trust the way he wouldn't look at her as he kicked at the debris on the floor. The color suddenly drained from his face. He dropped to his knees, rocked back and forth. "Oh my God. Oh. My. God."

He leaned forward. Sam watched his hands

shuffle through the debris, in the slow measured movements of someone not wanting to risk disturbing a dangerous adversary. With whatever he reached for cradled in his hands, he turned his face to look at her. Sam felt a chill run down her spine.

Without a word, he lifted his hands high enough to show what he held. High enough for the diamonds to catch and reflect back the light from the overhead bulb. The way the two of them stared at a fortune in diamonds, in the midst of the chaos of his rampage, on the floor of a cheap motel room, could have been a scene in a third-rate movie.

The jewels sparkled, beckoned, not with cold but with fire. In that instant, Sam had an uncomfortable understanding of why people would covet, steal or kill for the thrill of holding them. And she admitted Jerry Bellham had conceived an ingenious method to move stolen gems. No one would suspect a movie property manager of replacing false stones with authentic jewels until enough time had passed and the genuine product could be sold without notice.

"Damn," Christopher whispered. "They're here."

CHAPTER 3

HE DIDN'T KNOW what to do. His first impulse was to spread his hands wide apart, let the jewels fall to the floor. Then he thought he should close his fists tight and hold onto them. Any decision he made didn't change the circumstances.

He was in serious trouble

He'd stumbled upon a scene no notable director would have filmed. He'd watched life drain out of a man. That he hadn't cared for Tyler much added to the sick roiling in his stomach. Now he was being pursued as a suspect in that murder. And his mother cried on television. Christopher couldn't recall ever seeing his mother cry.

"Sam. I swear. I didn't know I had them."

She tilted her head and stared at him. "How could you not have felt them?" She gestured to the messenger bag discarded by his feet. "Didn't you notice the weight?"

"The scene calls for the bag having a gun tucked inside, so I didn't give it any thought."

"The scene you were going to rehearse with Tyler?"

"Yes."

"It was in your trailer?"

"Yes." He looked down at the fortune he held in his hands. The diamonds shone, but all he could see was the blood pouring out of Tyler's stomach, the glaze of death in his gaze, the whispered apology before he drew his last breath.

"After the meeting, I went to my trailer. I was pissed at Tyler about that scene he made at the end of the rewrite meeting. I tried cooling off in the shower. Ate a sandwich, had a beer. As I was getting ready to leave, I saw the bag peeking out from under the seat. Sure. I wondered how it got there, but props get dropped off all the time on set. I just figured someone who knew about the rehearsal had brought it by." He stared down at the bag. "Tyler must have come looking for this, and that's why he wasn't in his trailer. This is what he told Jerry he couldn't find. We must have taken different routes and that's why our paths didn't cross."

Which in all likelihood saved his life. He spread open his hands and the diamonds tumbled over his fingers onto the floor, landing on top of an unopened package of plain, white T-shirts.

"What do we do now?" he asked.

Sam knelt beside him and lifted the necklace. Christopher knew it was impossible, but it looked to him as if the diamonds glowed brighter, hotter, where they draped over her elegant fingers. He could picture her wearing them. And only them. It made no sense. Not only that he found himself tangled up in this real-life intrigue, but that he could have these thoughts about the woman beside him. The woman who'd taken it upon herself to believe and protect him.

She placed the necklace in the messenger bag, set it between them. He wondered if she did so as a ploy to see what he did. Or was it a sign of her trust?

She began sorting and stacking the discarded items. "So far no one's been able to locate us so we stay here. At least for tonight. That's why you can't contact your mother, Christopher." She looked at him. "I know it's hard for you to let her go on thinking something has happened to you, but we need to stay hidden as long as possible. I can promise the authorities and possibly Jerry's bad cops have her phone tapped in case you call."

"She calls me a couple of times a week," he said, his lips curving a little. "Says she wants to make sure I'm not getting full of myself and forget what's important."

"And that is?"

"Family. Mom's really big on family. She tries to have everyone over for dinner as often as possible." He sat a moment. "Yesterday she called to give me grief about my choice for this year's cookie list."

"Cookie list?"

"For Christmas. Every year everyone in the family gets to make a cookie request." He shrugged when Sam stared at him. "Most of the time we all ask for an old favorite, but sometimes there's a new cookie that someone has tasted. I had sent her a recipe I got from Janice in the Commissary for these square pretzels that you melt a piece of chocolate on, then add sprinkles."

"That doesn't sound like a cookie."

"That's what Mom said." Christopher grinned. "What's your favorite Christmas cookie?"

"I'm not much for Christmas."

"You spend the day with your family, though, right?"

She looked away. "No."

"Oh, I guess being with the Secret Service meant you didn't get to come home for Christmas much."

"My family's not like yours."

"Well, you're here in the states now. You'll come with me on Christmas."

She turned back, her eyes narrowed. "What?"

"To my parents' house. You'll come for Christmas. I have to warn you though, with an older brother and sister, their spouses, and a total of five nieces and nephews, plus my younger brother and his new wife, it gets loud and crazy at times."

"Don't be ridiculous." She started to rise, stopped when Christopher covered her hand with his, closing tight before she could pull away.

"I'd like for you to spend Christmas with me."

"Maybe you would," she said after a brief pause. "But I'm quite sure your Mother would have another opinion."

"Are you kidding? She'll love it. She's really

passionate about gender equality, or in her words inequality, so I warn you she'll be asking all kinds of questions about your job."

"No." Sam freed her hand, scrambled to her feet. "I don't mean she won't be interested in me because of my job."

"What then?"

Sam closed her eyes, as if fighting for patience. "Christopher, I'm flattered that you think you're attracted in me, and I admit I find you appealing."

He stood now, reached for her hand. Her eyes opened and he saw something like misery in her brown eyes. "I'm more than attracted, Samantha."

"The point is, maybe we could have indulged in an affair, but what you're talking about." She pressed her lips together. "I'm not the kind of woman you should take home to meet your family."

"Why not?" he asked. "Because you're intelligent? Because you're attractive? Because you're capable of taking down a 200-pound man?"

"You know none of that is what this conversation is about."

"Okay, then, tell me why you're nervous about meeting my family."

"It's not nerves," she said, throwing her hands

up in to the air. "It's the fact that I'm thirteen years older than you."

He gave himself the pleasure of taking a slow, thorough, look up and down her body. She wore black jeans, snug at the hips and formed to legs that were long and shapely. He skimmed back up, noted the tailored white shirt hanging loosely over a narrow waist, before rising to linger over small breasts.

"It's twelve years and five months to be exact," he corrected.

"Damn it, Christopher, be serious."

"I am."

He stepped closer, felt a little lift to his ego when she took a step in retreat. He considered crowding her a little more, but remembered she excelled in hand-to-hand combat. Not that he wouldn't mind a little hand-to-hand, or hand-to-any-other-body-part, but he got the impression she wasn't ready for that yet. Besides, it intrigued him that she was so resistant to meeting his family.

"Sam." How had he never realized how feminine that masculine shortened version of her name could sound? Or was it only because it applied to this particular woman? "I am serious about wanting you to meet my family." To hell with it, he took that step closer. "I am serious about wanting to be with you."

"I'm sure you are. As attractive as you are, Christopher, if I didn't like you, I wouldn't even consider being intimate with you." He felt his pulse ramp up but kept his gaze steady on hers, as hers was on his. "But I also realize I'm a bit of a novelty for you. That would be fine, something we could each enjoy, if not for this situation." With a slow indrawn breath, she took a step back. "I can't help you, can't protect you, if I let emotion take control of my actions and decisions."

As much as he enjoyed hearing her voice her attraction, along with the worry that it could overpower her logic, something else she said pissed him off.

"You're no novelty to me." In a quick move he doubted she anticipated, he eased her into his arms. Not to prove her point about their attraction, not to show her how very much he wanted to get her into bed. Instead, he held her because he got the impression few if any people had ever taken the time or care to hold her for no reason beyond just holding her. She kept her body stiff, confirming his suspicion. Wanting to soothe, he rubbed a hand up and down her back.

"But you're right. Tonight's not the night for me to show you how much I want you." He pressed his lips, lightly, to her temple. "To have the time to show you all the ways I want you." He sighed and glanced around the room. "And hopefully, we'll have much nicer surroundings when I do."

"Oh, to be young and optimistic." She shook her head, took another step back. "Not that I ever had the luxury of being optimistic when I was young."

"What does that mean?"

"You don't want to know."

"Sam." He took her hand, preventing her from walking away. What was it about this woman that grabbed him?

On surface she came across as cool, contained and a bit of a hard-ass. He imagined some of that was the result of her profession. But, at times like this, and other times when he'd observed her interacting with others, a kind of lonely vulnerability mixed with suppressed longing told him there were pockets of emotion waiting to be discovered.

"I want to know everything about you," he said.

"We have nothing in common."

"Opposites attract."

"You're too stubborn for your own good."

"Focused." He leaned toward her, watched heat bring a new wicked light to her eyes. "You'll appreciate that once I touch you, make love to you."

"That," she said but he saw her pause, saw her throat work as she swallowed. "Would be a mistake."

"I don't think so."

"We need to be figuring out a course of action."

"You said yourself we should lay low tonight."

"You are the most arrogant young man I've ever met."

"Determined. And age has nothing to do with it."

He leaned in closer, slid his arms around her waist, preventing her from putting more distance between them. He didn't agree that this would be a mistake. Maybe he considered, for half a second, she might be right that they should be planning their next course of action. Only, he wanted this, needed her.

"Let me taste you, Samantha. Let yourself taste me."

She settled hand on his hips and in that small

gesture, he felt a jolting need unlike any he'd ever known. A strong woman, and God knew he believed Sam to be one of the strongest it was his pleasure to meet, seldom relented, rarely allowed herself to be taken under. But, with one brush of lips, and the following light sound in her throat, she allowed herself to be lead.

Determined to be careful, to have as much of her as she would allow, he went slow. It was no hardship even as it tortured him with hints of what it would be like to taste more than her lips.

Small brushes of mouth to mouth, a slow trace of her lips with his tongue. Then, when hers opened, invited, there was the smooth glide of tongues, the in and out motion that enticed and beckoned. Her body softened, warmed, as she leaned into his. Her hands went lax on his hips. He didn't doubt she'd shove him away in a heartbeat if he went too far, too fast. Not because she didn't want him. No woman kissed like this without desire pounding in her blood. No, Samantha would push him away because he had been able to unlock the chain she usually kept on her passions.

He thought it incredibly sad that no one had recognized how much she needed to be cared for, treated with soft passion as much as with heated responses.

No other woman he'd ever been with had been as generous with a kiss, as giving even as she held back. For that very reason he managed to choke back the urge to move them to the bed, to strip off that reserve along with her clothes and plunge deep inside her. To do so now would limit them to a single time, a fast coupling rooted in circumstances as much as need and passion. Afterward she'd view it as a mistake.

When he made love to her, and he would, she wouldn't be in a hurry or have regrets.

Aching for her, he drew away. She opened her eyes and a depth of emotion urged him to take her mouth again, a dark need that said she'd accept him if he did more than kiss her. Because he also glimpsed a thin thread of panic beneath all that emotion and need, he resisted the temptation.

"I've wanted to do that since the day you came on set."

"It changes nothing."

"It sure changed something for me." He had to bite the inside of his mouth when her brows knitted. "I'm not going to be as patient now, Sam. But

I'm also not going to ask you for more tonight." Unable to resist, he leaned forward and pressed a kiss to that line between her brows. His life was a mess right now, but he felt confident that the woman in front of him would find a way to prove him innocent. And if, along the way, he talked her into bed, so much the better.

"Why don't you shower first?" He grinned when he glanced over at the bed. "After, we can discuss which side you like best."

SAM PRESSED her forehead against the slick wall of the shower. A stream of unflattering curses ran through her mind with more vigor than the water pissing out of the showerhead. She hated that Christopher had gotten under her skin enough to have her resort to cursing. If people asked anyone who knew Sam, who'd worked with her, they'd tell you she only cursed in the most extreme situations.

God knew everything she'd gone through today was extreme. Starting with being held by Christopher as she walked him through the scene this morning. She'd admired his body, but those strong hands, and the surprise that they weren't manicure soft, had held her with a gentleness that had her straining not to lean into him. It had been more difficult than she could have imagined to step free of him, to break her gaze from his.

He'd startled her when he found her outside Sadie's trailer, impressed her with the way he'd held it together as he related what he'd seen and heard. Then he'd proved helpful as they hurried across the studio lot. He'd been charming as they shopped at the discount store. The only time he'd broken was when he watched his mother on the news.

She shook her head, began lathering shampoo in her hair. That response, that level of caring, had crushed the dam on his fear. And because it had, they'd discovered the diamonds.

Seeing the stunned look on his face when he cradled a fortune in diamonds, there could be no doubt about Christopher's innocence in the theft and murder. But there had certainly been nothing innocent about that kiss. Her hair rinsed, she slid the disposable razor up the length of her right leg.

She'd guessed he would be a good kisser. What

had staggered her was how she'd had to battle against the need to tug him closer, take the kiss deeper. They were basically on the run from the police and whoever wanted the diamonds. Now was not the time to get distracted by kisses and the desire for more. If she lost focus, if she allowed her thoughts to center on Christopher as a man rather than as someone in need of protection, you ran the risk of someone getting hurt.

She'd allowed it to happen once before. She couldn't let it happen again.

SHE'D BEEN awake for nearly five minutes but had yet to move, keeping her breathing slow and steady. It was selfish, no doubt foolish, but she wanted to enjoy the sensation of being held, as if cared for, as long as it lasted. Because then, she'd again have to be hard and on guard.

But for now, she could be soft and vulnerable. Feminine. Desired.

Christopher curled against her back. Because they both had slept in boxers, she with a T-shirt, he with nothing, she felt the warmth of his skin and the rock-hard muscles of his chest and stomach.

And, she bit down on her tongue to keep the moan from escaping, an impressively hard morning erection pressed to the seam of her ass. His arm curved over her waist, with a hand spread over her stomach. She thanked her daily workout routine that he didn't handle too much excess weight.

When she'd exited the bathroom last night, she'd discovered he'd straightened the clutter, piling packages in a neat order. While he'd showered, and she'd failed trying not to picture him gloriously naked and wet, she'd settled on the narrow bed. As silly as it sounded, she'd tucked the bag of diamonds under her pillow. He'd joined her without a word. Until she clicked off the bedside lamp.

"Thank you for sticking by me today, Sam," he'd whispered into the darkness.

She could have excused her behavior as instinctive, which it had been at times, or could have simply ignored the comment. Only, he'd said her name in that way he had of making it sound intimate. Plus, she knew how lonely it was to believe yourself abandoned in a horrible situation.

"I'm with you until we get this mess straightened out."

Which, she rationalized, was another reason to

lay here a little longer. She had to decide the best course of action for today. There was no question she'd contact Hank. As long as her name stayed out of any connection with Christopher, and she didn't expect that to hold much longer, she could continue to use her phone. She'd used her credit card last night at the discount store but thought it best to avoid doing so again. They'd need another car, one that didn't require stealing or swapping license plates.

"You have a bad habit of hogging the covers."

She nearly jumped at the unexpected interruption to her thoughts. Then, she fought the shudder when he brushed aside her hair so he could press his lips to the top of her shoulder. His arm tightened, holding her still.

"I'm not in the habit of sharing."

"Ever? Or recently?"

She might have shrugged, had he not been pressed so close. Instead she closed her eyes and soaked up this last little bit of indulgence. And tried really hard not to think of whispered conversations between lovers in the early morning light.

"Not in a while."

Before he could press for more, her cell chimed. Reaching to the charger on the night table had his hand slipping away. Not recognizing the number on the screen, she frowned as she clicked to accept the call. Before she could say anything, a male voice came over the receiver.

"Is this Samantha Ethridge?"

"Who is this?" she demanded rather than acknowledge.

"We know you're with Christopher Reardon. And we know he's got the diamonds." Sam scrambled to sit. She switched on the light, saw that it was four minutes shy of eight. "Have you watched the news yet this morning? Do it. We'll be in touch."

"Turn on the television," she said to Christopher when the line went dead. "The news."

He didn't ask why. That should have been her first clue. With a few clicks, the screen showed a reporter, standing in front of a police station, sounding somber as he began his report. In a small corner box was a photo of another man.

"The police have no new updates on the death of our colleague. From phone records they have confirmed his time of death was two hours after he reported having received a phone call from Christopher Reardon. As reported earlier, the actor called in to plead innocent against the accusations of his involvement in the death of his co-star Tyler Collins."

Sam jumped out of bed, spun around to stare at Christopher.

"What the hell did you do?"

CHAPTER 4

CHRISTOPHER ROLLED out of bed and faced her. His stance, and the way his hands curled into fists at his sides, projected defiance.

"I defended myself against the lies that I stole a fortune in diamonds and I killed a man." His fists relaxed and flexed tighter. "I called that reporter and asked him to contact my mother and reassure her that I'm alive. I didn't call her."

"No, but the man you contacted is dead."

Christopher paled. "My mother."

Sam wanted to go to him, hold him, reassure him nothing had happened to his mother – yet – or that would have been part of the newscast. Instead she focused on what needed to be done next.

"Because you called the reporter, whoever is looking for you tracked him down and was able to trace your call back to my phone." She moved to the bed, drew the bag of diamonds from underneath her pillow. "Get dressed. We've got to get out of here."

"Sam." He rounded the bed, reached for her, let his hand drop when she stepped back. "I'm sorry."

"I told you to make no calls."

"You said my mother's line would be monitored. This was to the news station."

"And you think calls there aren't monitored?"

"I . . . I didn't think."

She considered, and immediately rejected, throwing out that of course he didn't think because he was young. He didn't have the years of experience she did. He'd been raised by good people who'd taught him to believe the best in everyone. He worked in a damned fantasy world where the only bad things that happened to people were make believe and resolved within a specific time frame.

The phone chimed, breaking the silence. Picking up the lamp on the bedside table, she broke the phone screen, slammed again until the phone broke into pieces.

She shucked down her boxers, drew on jeans. "Look, I might not have the same kind of base you do, but I get how important your family is to you." She zipped, drew a T-shirt and bra out of one of the backpacks they'd bought. "I've been trained to handle these kinds of situations. There are reasons why I tell you to do, or not do, something. I have to be able to trust you, Christopher, every bit as much as you trust me."

"I do trust you."

"As an actor you know how words can be slanted to fit a purpose," she said, hating to be cruel. But she couldn't back down. His welfare as much as her heart demanded she present a solid front. Still, if she understood that, accepted that, why did she still struggle against crossing the room and holding him? Have him hold her? With a shake of her head, she walked to the bathroom.

"Get dressed," she said. "We don't have much time."

They didn't speak as they dressed and packed up their meager belongings. Without discussion, Sam looped the messenger bag over her shoulder. After a careful study of the parking lot, she gave a nod and they went to the car. Once they got coffee and a breakfast biscuit from a drive-thru some the tension between them eased.

"I won't make a mistake like that again," Christopher said.

She glanced over, saw his untouched biscuit on his lap. Lifting her go cup, she drank the strong coffee. "As soon as I can buy a burner phone, I'll reach out to my boss and have him send someone over to see about your family."

"I would appreciate it."

She tried, and failed, to accept this stiff tone. "Look, I know I was hard on you." Silence as he continued to stare out the windshield, a hand wrapped around the paper cup of his coffee. "I was frightened." She sighed as the words escaped. From the corner of her eye she saw him look over. There were a couple of ways she could get around her unexpected confession. She could relate some event she'd seen or been involved with while in the Secret Service. Or she could reveal the one incident that had changed her life.

After all, if she expected his trust, she had to offer her own.

"I haven't mentioned that I grew up in Los Angeles."

"No, I didn't know."

She darted a glance in the rear-view mirror, frowned when a car, dark blue and three cars back, looked familiar. "My mother left when I was four. Maybe because I was so young, or maybe because I chose not to, but I don't remember her. I don't know why she left, my father never said. He worked night at the docks, slept during the day, so I went to day care or school."

"And nights?" Christopher asked when she paused while glancing before switching lanes.

"Babysitters when I was young, kept an eye on myself when I got older."

"Define older."

She looked over, surprised by his demand.

"I'm not sure, I think around eight."

"You were a child."

"See?" She took one hand from the steering wheel, pointed it at him. "That's what I'm trying to explain to you, why it's impossible to act on this foolish infatuation you have. Even if there wasn't the age difference, our lives have nothing in common."

"Plenty of people have nothing in common and manage to be together. My parents do."

"What?" She looked at him long enough that a

car honked at the way she'd slowed down. "What are you talking about?"

"My father's an accountant and likes nothing better than spending hours at home reading with a single brandy at his elbow. He's the spitting image of the buttoned-up, introverted bookworm. My mother is the managing partner in a construction firm. She's the managing partner because she spent years hammering and sawing on construction sites. She's loud, not afraid to voice her opinion, and does so often, and is more comfortable in jeans than in a dress."

"You said she bakes cookies."

"Yeah, and trust me, it's the only thing she's allowed to do in the kitchen."

"You're making that up." She thought of the woman crying in front of a camera. That was not a woman who worked in a male-oriented field, ordering about laborers on a daily basis.

"You'll see for yourself when you come over Christmas day. Eight years old?" he asked to get her back to her story. "How did you manage that by yourself?"

"It was all I knew." A quick look in the rear-view showed plenty of traffic but she didn't see the car she'd suspected of following them. "My father had to work so I kept to myself. Then, when I was fourteen, everything changed. I still don't know why, but one day a girl in school, a grade older, sat beside me in the cafeteria. We became friends." Because her throat wanted to close, she forced the words out, fast and sharp.

"I guess you could say Lucia took me under her wing. One night we were walking back from the movies when these three boys started following us. At first they said things soft and friendly." She had to sip some coffee.

"It didn't stay that way," Christopher guessed.

"No. Over her shoulder Lucia told them we didn't want anything to do with little boys. The words were barely out of her mouth when they dragged us into this alley. One of them back-handed Lucia, tore open her blouse. I." She swerved the car, a blasting horn indicated how close they'd come to an accident, and pulled into a strip shopping center. She made it to an isolated space at the rear of the center before she braked to a stop.

"One of the boys held me with an arm around my throat. One held Lucia onto the ground while the other." She sucked in a breath, tried to calm her racing heart. "He unbuckled his belt. Lucia fought hard enough that he called to the boy holding me, yelled for him to help hold her down. Lucia looked me in the eye, screamed at me to run. And I ran."

"Christ, Sam." Christopher undid his seat belt, started to scot closer. She hunched her shoulders in rejection of his kindness.

"She was beaten, raped brutally and often, then left to die. Alone, in an alley. Because I ran."

"It's not your fault."

"I ran," she repeated. "Not to the cops, not to anyone who might have helped her. I ran home, shut myself into our apartment and cried in the dark."

"You were what? Fourteen?"

"Not after that day." The trembling had all but stopped, her breathing came easier. "I swore never again would I let someone die trying to protect me." She looked at him, then was thankful she'd taken the time. "Shit. Get down."

"What?" He turned to look out his window. She shoved his head down to his knees, followed suit just as a shot blasted the window. Tiny pieces of glass scattered over them.

Thankful she hadn't shut down the engine, keeping her head below the dashboard, she put the engine in gear and floored the accelerator. The car bounced, skidded, as it hit a parked truck before she straightened it out. Another shot rang out, pinging off the rear fender. Sam dared to sit up a little, kept her gaze steady through the thin gap between the upper rim of the steering wheel and the car hood. With a break barely large enough for the car, she veered into traffic.

She sat up a little more, looked in the rear-view. Saw the dark sedan she'd spotted earlier, four cars behind them. Along with the driver was another person, one who cast a wide shadow, indicating he was a big man. She and the driver tailing them had slowed, hoping to avoid the wrong kind of attraction. The obliterated passenger window wouldn't help her cause.

"This is what I get for allowing personal feelings to interfere," she muttered.

"How the hell did they follow us?" Christopher demanded.

"Stay down," she answered when he lifted his head.

"Not a chance." She flicked him a glance, was met with a pissed-off look in return. "I'm not letting you take shots for me."

Spotting a parking garage, she continued straight ahead. The car trailing them moved up a car closer but continued with the same cautious speed as she did. Scanning the surroundings, she spotted a place advertising no-contract cell phones placed perfectly between a souvenir shop and a sandwich shop. Ahead she saw the stoplight change from green to red. Swerving around a slowing car, she sped up, darting through the intersection. She grinned when, with a quick look in the rear-view, she saw the tailing car had no choice but to stop at the light behind a law-abiding driver. Taking a series of turns they ended up on the road where they'd left the trailing car behind.

"What are you doing?" Christopher asked.

"We've got to ditch this car." She pulled into the parking garage she'd spotted earlier, circled the levels, heading for one closer to the top before sliding into a space. She reached for both backpacks, rooted through hers to find the package of baby wipes. She pulled one two, handed them to Christopher. "Wipe down anything you touched." They worked quickly and silently. It impressed and pleased her that she didn't have to explain to wipe off the handle after he exited the car.

"Now what?"

She heard the excitement in his voice, saw the glint of adrenaline in his eyes. That worried her.

Too much was every bit as dangerous as too little. She needed to find an outlet, to calm him before they went on the street. Not questioning if it was self-serving or not, she grabbed a fistful of his shirt and tugged him hard enough that the force had her back slamming against the concrete wall. She felt his backpack slip out of his hand, drop onto her foot, an instant before those hands gripped her hips. Their mouths met, skimmed. Then took in a frantic need that reached deep inside Sam and released a passion unlike any she'd ever known.

It was a kiss that swamped the senses. She forgot where they were, why they were there, why she'd made the move in the first place. All that mattered, all she wanted in the world, was to continue kissing him. Then he cupped a hand around her breast and she knew she couldn't stick with just kissing much longer. Even as the wild hunger shifted into something that enticed rather than consumed, a low pulsing that demanded her to cherish what she enjoyed, she found it impossible to step away.

She wanted this. Wanted him. Forgotten, ignored, dismissed, were all the reasons why it wouldn't work. All she knew, all she felt, was the joy of knowing this man wanted her. Yes, a small part of her brain acknowledged the situation, the danger they'd just escaped, the threats still to be faced. Only, for once, because it was Christopher, she took this small break from reality and indulged her heart.

Until his kisses slowed the desperation, softened the force of his mouth on hers. And this, she realized, was the greatest danger. Passion, when coupled with speed, could be given and taken without care. But tenderness could never be ignored, should never be ignored. Even when it was the very reason for turning away.

"Well," she murmured against his lips. Her voice wasn't quite as cool as she'd wanted. And her mouth really wanted to once again be pressed to his. "That certainly took my mind off being shot at."

He flexed his hands, once, painfully, on her hips before they dropped free. He didn't step back, at least not physically, but distance separated them. It took every ounce of will she possessed to meet his gaze. His blue eyes were direct and calm. He's an actor, she reminded herself. He knows how to shield his personal feelings and give a performance.

"You've got that right." He picked up the fallen

backpack, again met her gaze. "We should get out of here." After a pause that was too long to be anything but deliberate, he took her hand. "Lead the way."

CHRISTOPHER HAD every intention of winning an Oscar someday. So far, every role he attempted, every part he won, had been chosen deliberately. Whether because of the storyline, or the director, or, in one case, the opportunity to film in Ireland, he'd made sure he learned a valuable lesson with each choice.

When he finally held that golden statue in his hands, when he knew the pride of earning recognition from his peers and the admiration of his family, he would remember this day. He would also recall how hard it had been to not rage at Sam's comment. The hurt couldn't be stopped, but it had been contained. Just he'd resisted the near overwhelming need to keep her against the wall and make love to her right then and there.

And how, given no other choice, he'd had to accept the barrier she erected between them.

"Wait."

When her hand squeezed his, he stopped before stepping free of the shelter of the building. Glancing down, he noted her knuckles were white.

"Christopher, I'm sorry." He looked at her face, saw the misery swimming in her brown eyes. "Please don't be mad with me. What I said was wrong."

"In what way?"

"I had to put some distance between us," she said, then drew in a breath. Looked away from him. "Otherwise I would have ignored everything we're caught up in and gotten back into that car, driven us to the nearest motel and asked you to make love to me."

"I was a breath away from taking you against the wall."

"See?" She jabbed a finger at him. "That's what I'm trying to tell you. We're wrong for each other."

"Wrong? Not a chance. The timing might be wrong. But." He took her in his arms, held her until her body slowly relaxed. "But," he murmured, "we're not wrong."

"I can count at least twenty different ways why we shouldn't be together."

"Name one. One," he hurried. "Other than age."

"I can't protect you the way you need if I'm thinking of getting you naked."

His lips curved as they nuzzled her throat. "Try again." His lips trailed up to nip at her chin. "You're a strong, capable woman, Sam. And that's just the start of why I'm attracted to you." He lifted his head to stare at her, at the intriguing combination of denial and acceptance in her brown eyes. "I have faith in you."

She hesitated and he could see the turmoil in her gaze. No doubt about it, it boosted his ego. But he also saw the resolute determination shut down the desire.

"Then let's get moving," she said.

He smiled when she kept his hand in hers as she led them down the interior stairway and out where they crossed the street at the crosswalk. He expected her to go straight for the phone, but instead she entered the souvenir shop.

"Looking for a map to the stars' homes?" he asked.

She ignored him, stopping long enough to grab a Dodger ballcap off a wall. Ripping the price tag off, she settled it on his head, low enough to shadow a portion of his face. "I'm not sure how much good this will do," she said in a low voice intended just for him as they walked to the cash register. "But hopefully it'll help you blend in."

"I'm an Angels fan."

She delighted him by grinning and patting his cheek. "Not when I'm paying."

She bought several phones and sent him into the sandwich shop for take-out subs while she stood on the sidewalk and made calls. He kept looking over his shoulder, watching her. It lessened some of his worry that she blended right in with so many walking by, almost all of them talking on a cell phone.

No, he corrected, she would never blend. At least not to him. Even knowing it was a factor of her job, past and current, to be in the background, his eye would always be drawn to her. Now that he'd had a taste of her passion, simmering below the surface just waiting to explode, he understood the sensuality in her every move and gesture. Just as he now had a better idea of the sadness, grief and regret in her eyes when she'd told him about her friend.

He appreciated now what guided her, what had been at the root of all that contained emotion. She'd needed to maintain control because at a young age, at a pivotal moment in her life, she'd had none. She'd dedicated her life to protecting others as a way to honor the friend who'd protected her.

He was willing to bet she used measured distance in every relationship rather than allow herself to get close enough to anyone for fear of being hurt or abandoned again.

She looked at the crowd around them as he joined her, pitched her voice low. "We've got a ride at a Dented Drives lot. We just need. . . " He swung her around and took her mouth in a deep, satisfying kiss. He heard a whistle and a complaint about them blocking the walkway. When he judged enough time passed, not that he hadn't enjoyed the diversion, he lifted his mouth just enough to speak.

"There was a cop car coming down the street. To be on the safe side, I figured he shouldn't get a look at our faces."

Because she was there, because he wanted, he skimmed her lips again. Her taste, her response, had him wishing they were alone in a dark room with nothing more demanding than the intimacy they could share. Would share.

"Instead, you've created a scene too many people will remember."

"All they'll see are a man and woman indulging in a little holiday affection."

"They'll pity a desperate older woman clinging to a younger man."

He tightened his hold when she tried to wiggle free. "Sam, there isn't a woman alive who'd ever see you as desperate." His lips caressed hers. "And every man, young or old, will think I'm one lucky bastard to have such a vibrant woman interested in me."

She broke free of his embrace and walked the few feet needed to wait for a bus. "This is a ridiculous conversation to have on the side of the road. We need to get to the car."

He followed her, stood beside her as they waited, sat hip-to-hip beside her once they were on the bus. He considered arguing with her about the way she'd dismissed what he saw as the inevitability of them becoming lovers. He wanted to protest the way she'd tossed her own worth and strength aside. He especially resented the fact that she used the flimsy excuse of age.

But he kept quiet, doing nothing to convince nor antagonize her. After all, he accepted her wish for them to go as unnoticed as possible. Once they were on the road, once they had little choice but to find another cheap motel for the night . . . then, he'd used every word, touch, and kiss at his disposal to show her just how right they were together.

He pulled his cap lower on his forehead as he pretended to doze off. And to hide his smile.

CHAPTER 5

WITH TRANSPORTATION, a full tank of gas and cash hidden in various places, Sam drove aimlessly through Los Angeles. She really didn't have any experience in the kind of investigative process needed to prove Christopher's innocence. So, she'd agreed with Hank to let some of his crew do the necessary digging while she and Christopher kept a low profile.

Unfortunately for her peace of mind, not to mention the persistent low thrum of lust curling in her belly, that meant the two of them had to stay together.

Twenty-four seven.

"Did you get together with your dad much while you were with the Secret Service?

She didn't sigh as she realized she'd subconsciously driven to the pier district which was why he'd probably asked.

"He came to my high school and college graduations. He didn't have a computer so we stuck with rare phone calls."

"He never visited you at any of the countries where you were assigned?"

"No." She smiled, knowing the thought of traveling had never appealed to her father. "He died two years ago. A dock accident."

"I'm sorry, Sam."

"What I came to accept was my mother leaving wasn't what closed us off. He was always a loner. Even if he'd been an accountant." Her feeble attempt at humor gained her a steady stare from him. "He'd be the kind who'd have stayed in his cube, done his work, and gone home at night to eat dinner in front of the television. He wasn't the kind to go out to a bar for after-work drinks with co-workers. And yes," she went on before he could comment. "I'm aware that many of my co-workers would say the same about me."

"Nothing wrong with being focused on your career. What made you quit?"

"I didn't quit, I took early retirement." Because

she'd listened to her heart rather than let training dictate her response. Thankfully the only loss had been her career.

"Okay."

"Retired," she repeating bristling a little at the humor in his agreement. "Because that's what older people do." How pathetic she'd become, using a transparent excuse to hold him at arm's length.

"My dad told me about this kid, seven, the studio hired," he said, stretching out his long legs as best he could in the footwell. "He was the main character voice for a limited run television cartoon series. The up-front pay wasn't all that much, but his mother, well we'll say she saw the potential, the long-term potential of that little show. She brokered with the studio for a guarantee that her little boy would receive a royalty percentage every time it aired. The studio brass didn't anticipate the audience reaction being so strong so they thought it was a no-brainer. You could say he retired before he reached thirteen."

"It's not the same."

"No, it's not. And I'm not trying to downplay you and your career. What I'm saying is you're still working, although in a different venue, and last I heard he spends his days sailing around his private beach and playing poker when the sun sets. Retirement can come at any age. For a variety of reasons." He grinned. "Since my dad's an accountant, I was raised hearing about finances and preparing for the future."

"I'm not sleeping with you because I want to feel young."

"Okay." He sat up, leaned over as far as the seat belt would allow and skimmed a fingertip down her cheek. She felt the touch down to her toes. "I'm just happy to hear you're going to sleep with me."

"I never said I would," she answered quickly. They both knew she lied. "I've wondered."

"So have I. And I have a feeling my fantasizes are going to fade into oblivion once we're together."

"I'm nothing like the young women you've been with."

"I haven't been with as many women, young or otherwise, as you think." He again slid his finger over her cheek. "Sam, you're more than the promise of a quick roll on the sheets to me."

She resisted the urge to rub at the ache between her breasts. They talked as if them becoming lovers was inevitable. Although there didn't seem to be any reason to pretend otherwise.

She appreciated the way he tried to reassure her, the tone of his voice, the look in his eye that promised he meant what he said. It changed nothing, nothing other than reassure her she could trust him to be gentle when they parted.

She could make another attempt at shutting him out. A wasted attempt, she decided as he shifted back to his side of the car. Right or wrong, she wanted to be with him. Age didn't matter, lifestyles and status made no difference, the past and present would be ignored while they were together. Even the circumstances wouldn't hold them back for long.

During the day, she could maintain an emotional if not actual physical distance while keeping an eye on their surroundings. It was once they stopped for the night, in a cramped room with little to no breathing room between them that she knew would break through her resolve to resist him. Perhaps if she made the decision, the move, to them becoming lovers, she could control the end of the affair.

Compounding the attraction, that gut-level hum of desire, was the fact that she liked him.

Pretty much had from their first meeting. So, she'd dodged and evaded, using whatever excuse came to mind. Until she no longer wanted to hide behind pretense.

Not that being on the run from suspicion of theft and murder weren't good excuses. In fact, as far as she was concerned, it was better for her ego that no one could watch from the sidelines as they became lovers. She didn't want to be the subject of gossip, or, worse, pity. Many people stroked their ego by turning to someone younger as they faced wrinkles and gray hair in the mirror.

While her ego didn't need a boost, she hoped to safeguard her heart with the same fierce tenacity she would use to protect Christopher.

"I think we should head out of the city," Sam said, darting another glance in the rear-view mirror.

"I'm with you on whatever you think is best," Christopher said, with an easy confidence. He leaned over, switched on the radio. It didn't surprise her when he settled on a station playing Christmas carols. It didn't even surprise her to hear him singing along.

"I bet you sang in the church choir."

"You'd lose," he said. "High school, after

Heather Wright suggested I try out for the chorus. Once I made it, however, she broke my heart by giving hers to the senior football quarterback."

"You're just full of stories, aren't you?"

He opened one eye to look at Sam. "Who's your great lost love from high school?"

"Didn't have one."

"There must have been someone you noticed, someone you dreamed about being with."

"Not in high school."

"Aha. Later then. College? No, I bet you were too focused then. Another agent?"

Images of an explosion, the dust and mayhem that followed. The blood and cries of the injured. The shouts of orders, the struggle to secure officials. The desperation of a man, a man who'd claimed to be falling in love with her, freeing the woman she learned he'd also been making claims and promises to.

The shame of what she viewed as a weakness had haunted her rigid code of ethics. Still, she'd told no one of that momentary lapse of judgement, had been relieved no death occurred as a result of her hesitation. No one had questioned her report. Instead, they'd commended her quick action in securing the safety of everyone in the embassy. There'd been talk of a promotion.

Having learned a hurtful lesson, Sam had taken early retirement and moved to Montana. Never again would he put her heart ahead of duty.

"No," she softly said. "Not another agent."

Christopher must have caught the regret, the instinctive shut-down of emotion, in her answer because he didn't press for more. So, with the cheerful and sentimental music filling the car interior, she maneuvered through traffic and steered the car north on Highway 170. They both checked the mirrors often. Conversation came and went, with the brief silences as comfortable as the topics they discussed.

When she spotted a small motel, she flicked on the turn signal.

"We're stopping already?" Christopher asked.

"I thought we should get a room before the other travelers decide to stop for the night. Besides, it's not like we're in a hurry to get anywhere." She shrugged. "We could both use a little down time."

Once she paid for the room, with Christopher remaining in the car, she didn't park in front of their room. Instead, she turned back and drove the short mile to bring them to a stop in front of a small Mexican restaurant with a covered patio.

"I want some fresh air, a cold beer and spicy salsa," Sam told Christopher, slipping the messenger bag filled with a fortune of diamonds over her shoulder as she looked at him over the roof of the car. She'd be taking a chance at someone recognizing him. However, the restaurant was off the beaten path and she thought the hat did a good job of camouflaging his features. So far there'd been no mention of her in any of the news reports they'd heard on the radio as they drove.

He grinned. "I knew you were the woman for me."

Her heart jumped, but it didn't worry her. It was a natural physical response to a good-looking man with a seductive smile. They made their way to a far corner of the patio beneath a faded umbrella, placed their orders. On the opposite corner, an inflatable Santa wore a sombrero rather than the traditional red cap. The air was dry, the beer was cold, the salsa like fire on the tongue.

"Do you miss Montana?" Christopher asked. "The cold?"

"I miss the quiet." She looked over the highway,

at the constant drum of traffic, then to the other tables on the patio. Three women, co-workers from what she'd overheard from their conversation, sat at one, while a teenage couple, definitely interested only in each other, sat at another. "I miss the countryside."

"What's your house like?"

"Your typical cabin, three bedrooms, a galley kitchen, open living room with the requisite wide window overlooking the barn. I don't have much land, a little less than ten acres."

"Barn? You have horses?"

"Two. I got them from a nearby ranch that works with wounded veterans." She relished the cold of her beer. "I've been thinking of getting a dog."

"I can picture you there." His eyes were fixed on hers. "I'd love to visit you there."

She managed to swallow without choking, but the beer burned rather than chilled as it slid down her throat. She didn't doubt he was sincere. That was the problem. How could she have an affair with him, even knowing the danger that kind of intimacy could bring to this protective detail, if he talked of afterward?

She was thankful for the training that kept her

face calm, her voice level. Still, in that moment, their surroundings faded, giving her a clear image of him, silhouetted by the mountains as he rode one of her horses. The all-too vivid image of him standing in her house, eating at her small table, feeding wood in the fireplace. Sleeping in her bed.

Although she didn't believe he'd ever make the trip, she knew those fleeting visions of him being there beside her would haunt her when she returned.

"Sure." She sipped the beer, praying it went down. "Next time you need to research a cowboy role, let me know and I'll pencil you in on my calendar."

He reached for her hand when she set down the mug, opened his mouth to say something. Words, promises, he had no business saying and she was better off not hearing. She couldn't open her heart to something kept silent. Sam let her breath gust out with relief when the waitress appeared with their meal.

"This looks amazing," she said, drawing her hand away to pick up her fork. Thankfully, he didn't press the issue of visiting her. They resumed their earlier easy conversation, drank more beer to cool down the tangy spice of good food. They laughed, but softly so as not to call any unwanted attention.

And, finally, as the last drop of beer rolled down the side of the mug, after the dishes had been cleared and the sun faded on the horizon, it was time to leave.

They drove in silence, gathered their backpacks of meager belongings. At the door of the motel room, Sam slid the key card into the slot, drew in a breath and walked inside, locking the door behind her.

Disappointment ripped through her at the discovery of two beds. There would be no excuse to indulge the luxury of waking with Christopher holding her close.

"Home sweet home." His voice came over her shoulder, reinforcing that lost sensation of him curled up behind her. He walked past, dropped his backpack and hat to the ground and stretched out on the bed farthest from the door.

She studied him. He looked relaxed, although she could see the ridge of muscle in his abs, in the arms he'd curled to pillow his head. His eyes were closed, his lips curved in a half-smile and his jaw showed he hadn't taken the time to shave that morning.

She considered walking over, could clearly picture herself stripping as she did so, as she straddled his hips. She could imagine sliding her hands under his shirt, feeling the hard planes of his stomach. And below. She practically trembled with the need to follow through, to let blood already warm go hot and fierce, to indulge this need he created within her.

As if reading her mind, his eyes opened, held her still. "Do you trust me, Sam?" he quietly asked, his voice carrying the shadow of vulnerability she'd glimpsed in his gaze.

"Yes." She pressed her lips together. She didn't tremble, but she felt the heat spark to life in her center, rise up within her. "Christopher."

He rose from the bed, crossed to her. Gently, he pried her fingers free of her backpack, tossed it onto the dresser. Using only fingertips, he lifted the messenger bag off her shoulder. He didn't toss it, instead he placed it on the small table between the beds.

"Everything is uncertain. Some people would say we did nothing more than find what little peace or security we could by being with each other." He turned so quickly she jolted. His eyes were a brilliant blue, blazing with need. "We've been drinking. I don't want to take advantage of that."

"Tonight was the first drink I've had in more than a year." She nearly smiled. "I'd made my decision before we went to that restaurant."

"Good." Only he didn't move.

"Don't make this out to be more than it is, Christopher. It's just two people wanting to lose themselves in good, strong sex."

Need warred with anger in his gaze. "What's between us is more than that."

No, it wasn't, couldn't be. But she didn't argue. She didn't want to argue. Better to show him how it was to be between them.

She went to him, stroking her hands down his chest so she could tug the T-shirt free of his jeans.

"I've never wanted a man the way I want you," she whispered, her lips cruising over his throat, up to his jaw, around to nibble at his ear. "I've never needed a man the way I need you."

The first thrill ran up her spine when his hands closed tight on her hips. Yes, this is what she wanted, depended on. To keep everything between them at a physical level

"Let me show you," she said.

"No." He cupped her face, lowered his mouth to

hers and gently tempered the raging urgency in her. That's when she knew he wouldn't let her rush this, wouldn't allow her to use the passion between them as a shield against the softer longings. He was going to undermine her reserve by using patience and tenderness.

"Let me show you," he said.

CHAPTER 6

IF GOING THROUGH ALL the fear, shock and disbelief of the last twenty-four hours plus meant having Samantha Ethridge in his arms, responding to his kisses, Christopher would do it all again.

During those hours he'd learned more about the woman, more than the fact that she was, without a doubt, the sexiest woman he'd ever known. Sex appeal was easy. If someone didn't have it, God knew there were plenty of doctors willing to nip, tuck, stretch or tone someone into achieving it. For Sam, it was an intrinsic part of her, one of those rare women who had it but didn't use it for her own advancement. But getting to know her better as they escaped and evaded had bumped up his attraction to her.

Even now, as her mouth parted for his kisses, as she arched into his caressing hands, as she made low accepting noises, she did so without pretense, without expecting anything more than a physical release in return.

He intended to give her far more.

His thumbs caressed her cheekbones as he took the kiss deeper. Still soft but with a hint of the heat and speed to come.

She didn't surrender. Of course not. Unlike some women he'd been with, younger and with an agenda of their own, Sam didn't give him complete control.

At least not yet.

It wasn't a battle, not even a skirmish. It was the first steps of a dance, an offering, the sharing of self, of need, of desire. Of trust. Her hands mirrored his, coasting up and down sides, backs. Only his stopped when they came upon the bump of the gun holster at the small of her back.

She stilled, her mouth drew away. Her eyes opened, questioning, wary.

"I'm looking forward to stripping you," he said, catching her bottom lip between his teeth. "But I'm not ashamed to say I'd feel better if you handle this one detail."

Relief came and went in her eyes, quickly followed by her stepping back, putting distance between them. Her hands hung by her side, making no move in any way.

"Does it bother you?" she asked.

"How could it when it's part of what brought you to me?"

Her eyes closed, her throat worked as she swallowed words. He wanted to hear them, wanted her to tell him everything she felt. Everything she wanted. Not just tonight.

He waited, unsure whether or not he'd said the wrong thing. It reminded him of being a boy of four filled with expectation as he waited to tell Santa what he wanted for Christmas while battling fear of sitting on the lap of a stranger with a big, booming voice.

Silently she lifted the hem of her shirt, reached behind her and unclipped the holster. She placed it on the bedside table next to the bag of diamonds. Then, to his surprise, she knelt down, reached under the leg of her jeans and freed the gun strapped there. When it joined the pile, she turned, her hands at the buttons of her shirt.

"Nope." He moved to her, covered her hands

with his. Smiled. Kissed her. "This is where I take the lead."

Keeping his gaze locked with hers, seeing the faint light of an authenticity he believed she rarely shared with another. That she did so now, with him, was humbling. It made him more determined than ever to go slow. Be thorough. With a shallow breath he skimmed a fingertip between the shirt he'd opened. Her skin was warm, soft. Leaning forward, he pressed his lips to the spot he'd uncovered, lingering, tasting.

He continued kissing, discovering as he moved up her throat, nipped at her jaw, covered her mouth with his. She moved her arms to curl around his neck.

Though it cost him, he kept the kiss soft, caressing rather than demanding. It aroused nonetheless. He eased the shirt off her shoulders, let it fall to the floor before he released the clasp of her bra. He hooked a fingertip in the material, drew it slowly away, exposing her breasts to his gaze. To his mouth.

His tongue circled the dark nipple, hardened it with quick flicks. Her breath caught and she gripped his hair, holding him in place when he sucked her deep into his mouth. Her hips arched against him, a silent plea for more. He paused only long enough for her to lift his shirt off before he worked down the zipper of her jeans, brushed the back of his knuckles against responsive skin.

When her hands sought to return the favor he stood still, torn between wanting the relief of having his jeans unzipped, wanting the torture of having her wrap a hand around him, yet knowing he didn't risk her touching him yet.

He wanted more, much more, than a quick release. For both of them.

With his mouth returning to kiss her, he angled down, caught the thin bedspread and flung it back. Gently he guided her to the bed, fit himself and his iron hard erection in the cradle of her thighs. His hands stroked, caressed. Her hips lifted, demanding, enough so that sweat broke out on his back.

"Easy," he whispered, his mouth trailing down to her breasts, enjoying the taste and feel of her filling his mouth before he continued down her torso. Rearing back, when those hips again lifted, he eased down her jeans. With a smile, he slipped a fingertip under the edge of her panties. She went still. Her gaze remained fixed on his and he could read the need, the edge of desperation he saw there. He saw the plea, one impossible to deny her.

He slid a finger inside her, groaned at the heat, wet heat, he found. He stroked, once, twice. On a ragged cry, she exploded around him.

He didn't cover her mouth to swallow, or share, her scream. Instead he let it echo in his head. And inside his heart.

When she went limp, he finished stripping her clothes. Then, he returned to that hot, wet center. Where he used his mouth to have her screaming again.

When she finally surrendered, when she simply lay there spread out like glory before him, he removed his clothes, rolled on a condom and settled between her thighs.

"Samantha." Her lids were heavy, giving him only a sliver of her brown eyes. Her cheeks were flushed, her mouth swollen from his kisses. And her cries of release. "There's no one like you. No one. No," he commanded when she started to lower her eyes. "Look at me and know who it is that's with you." He slipped inside, gritted his teeth against the snug way she closed around him, the way her hips curved up to take him deeper.

"Look at me and know that it's you I want to be with."

"Chris." The fingers of her right hand combed through his hair, brought his mouth down to hers.

He thrust, relishing the way her legs tightened around him, urging him. They moved together in a rhythm he'd never known possible. His moan of release joined hers as they climaxed together.

Collapsed on top of her, his breathing labored, Christopher enjoyed the soft relaxation of Sam beneath him. He felt pretty damned relaxed himself. Her hands coasted up and down his back, stirring a hunger he'd thought had been sated. Then, before he could decide on the best move to make, he found himself flipped onto his back.

Nothing could have delighted, or aroused, him more than Sam straddling his hips, using hers to shoot those first licks of new arousal into raging need. He expected to look up and find her smiling at him, maybe with some flirty challenge about her testing his stamina. Instead, he detected serious intent in her eyes.

"Samantha?" He levered up, wrapped his arms around her. She did the same to him, lowering her forehead to his chest. "What's wrong? Did I hurt you?"

"I should tell you it's wrong to be with you. But it's not." She rubbed against his chest. "I should regret this. But I don't." She skimmed her mouth under his jaw. "I should say it won't happen again. But I can't. I should say I don't want you again. But I won't." She clenched tight around him, arching her back a little. But her gaze stayed on his. "I do want you, Christopher. More than I should. But I can't resist you."

"No one's ever wanted me the way you do."

His declaration lowered a curtain on her expression. He knew she didn't believe him, unless it was to believe his words were a pretty lie between lovers. They were more, how much exactly more he wasn't sure. So, he said nothing more. Instead, he took her mouth, clouding his senses with the taste and response of her.

For now, until he could figure out what he wanted, he accepted the thrill and excitement of having a sensuous and giving woman drive him to distraction. And fulfillment.

SAM'S HEART hammered and she couldn't be sure her legs would hold her. While her body was slick with water, her mouth and throat were dry as dust. Bracing one hand on the vanity, she managed to step out of the tub. In a minute she'd find the energy to reach for a towel. Or, she could just stand here until she dried.

"That," she said, pausing to draw in a deep breath. "Shouldn't have been possible in that tiny excuse of a shower."

"You're one hell of an incentive, Sam."

From behind, Christopher wrapped his arms around her, held her against his chest. She could feel his heart pounding at her back.

She'd done that to him, she realized with pride. And not just this time. The first time they'd made love there'd been a sense of urgency. The second time, they'd gone slower, taken time to explore and exploit. The third time he'd given her full and complete control to do what she liked. Apparently, she liked a good deal more than she'd ever experienced. Then, this morning, when she'd barely limped her way into the shower, he'd joined her.

Somehow, she'd had energy each time they made love. And, God, it was a lovely bonus to know she'd given him equal satisfaction.

He'd told her no one had ever wanted him the way she did.

A part of her, a sliver of her heart, wanted to believe he meant more than sex. The reasonable side of her personality refused to put an emotional component to the words. Either way, she didn't have the time to puzzle it out. She still had the job of protecting him until his innocence could be proven. And the diamonds returned.

"Right now," she said, putting distance between them as she began to towel off. "The only incentive I'm interested in is food."

They were both reserved as they dressed and packed. Before leaving, Sam took the precaution of wiping down all surfaces and tying together the ends of the plastic bag lining the trash cans before stripping the bed and folding them and the linens into a ball. With a cautious glance out the door to insure no one spotted them, she threw the bundle into the back seat of the car.

"You've done that every time we left somewhere. Why?" Christopher asked, once they were headed out of town.

"C'mon, you've seen enough crime shows and movies to know we don't want to leave anything behind that can be connected to us."

"Are you sure that kind of caution is necessary?"

She looked at him. With no effort she could call to mind the way he'd looked while tenderly thrusting inside her. "I'm not willing to take the chance."

A few miles down the road, they found a truck stop diner that looked busy enough they wouldn't stand out. The bonus was the charity collection bin in the parking lot. Once she'd piled in the hotel linens, and the trash in the oversize can next to the door, they stepped into the hot sizzling air of bacon, pancake syrup and frying onions. A couple of men looked their way, turned back to their plates. One man, alone in a booth, studied them over the top of his paperback book. Sam didn't think he'd recognized them, but she kept her senses tuned to him.

It was the television hanging in a corner, tuned to a morning talk show, that worried her the most.

They'd no sooner settled in a booth when a waitress appeared. "Coffee?" she asked, even as she flipped over the thick white mug in front of Sam and began pouring.

"Thanks."

"You need time or do you know what you want?" she asked, smiling with a little flirtation mixed in with the question she directed at Christopher.

"Short stack," he said. "With a couple of eggs. Sunny side up, side of bacon."

"You've got quite an appetite."

He grinned at Sam. "Yes, I do."

She felt the fire on her cheeks, but turned her gaze to the waitress. "I'll have the same, only scramble my eggs."

"Be right out."

Sam followed the waitress walking away to check on the guy who'd watched them over the paperback. He'd gone back to his reading, so, relaxing a little, after a passing glance at the television, she reached for her coffee.

"Why haven't you had a drink in more than a year?"

She eyed him over the rim of her mug, considered. She could come up with any number of excuses or stories, could make them sound authentic. But the idea of being dishonest curled like sour milk in her stomach.

"My last assignment with the Service, I had a personal relationship that interfered with my ability to do my job." She drank coffee. "It hadn't yet turned physical, but we'd planned a weekend getaway." Setting down her mug, she looked Christopher straight in the eye. "He was, is, the assistant to the Ambassador. When shots rang out while they were outside the Embassy, I was slow to respond. In the end, I was able to get the Ambassador and her staff to safety. Not only did I have to face the reality that I nearly let my selfish hesitation result in the loss of a life, but I learned the man I was thinking of having an affair with, was in fact having one with the Ambassador."

She ran a fingertip up and down the handle of the mug. "It dented my female pride to know I was little more than another conquest, but what bothered me more is how I let my ethics slide, even for a second, when I considered personal feelings above duty."

"Here you go."

Sam and Christopher both leaned back a little to allow the waitress room to settle their plates before them. Along with the bill. "I'll be right back to refill your mugs."

She reached for the salt shaker, only to stop when Christopher covered her hand with his. "He didn't deserve you."

"Lesson learned." Both in terms of believing she was lovable and a reminder to keep her focus on the job at hand. She slipped out of his grasp, shook salt on her eggs. "When I left the Service, really for the first time since I'd been fourteen, I had time on my hands." She scooped up a bite of eggs. "I started with a glass of wine with dinner, then two, while cooking. I can still recall my shock the night I polished off an entire bottle by myself. You should eat before your breakfast gets cold," she said, pointing her fork at him.

"I never reached the point of needing a drink. I just got into the habit of it, and, even as I continued with that nightly drinking, I worried it was an easy habit to continue."

"What changed?"

"Nothing drastic, just one day I decided to try not to have that drink while cooking dinner. The next night, the same, along with skipping the drink with dinner." She spread butter between layers of her short stack, poured a skinny serving of syrup. "That became the habit."

"You're the strongest woman I've ever met."

She paused as the waitress topped off their coffee. Oh, that kind of compliment was hard to ignore or dismiss. Harder to not press close to her heart. She reminded herself that they were together under unusual circumstances.

"Christopher, you're used to young girls consumed with appearance, social media, and meeting the right people. I'm older, stay in the background as much as possible due to personality as much as vocation, and consider only a select handful of people as friends."

She looked away from him, zeroed in on the television. "Well, hell," she muttered, low, while she stared at her photo on screen. And yet a small part of her was grateful for the diversion. "And now I'm a person of interest."

She gulped coffee. "We've got to get out of here. No," she said, when he started to slide out of the booth. "We can't rush out. It'll draw too much attention." She scanned the room. "Hardly anyone's looking at the television. Take a few more bites." She did the same. "Then make your way to the restrooms in the back. I'll wait three minutes before I leave. I'll drive around to pick you up." She reached for his hand, squeezed hard. "Don't take any risks."

He smiled at her, and either he was more worried than he wanted her to know, or she'd gotten good at reading him, but she saw the nerves in the curve of his lips. Still, using the pretense of normalcy, he ate a slice of bacon and a couple of bites of pancakes, followed by a swallow of coffee. "Be right back," he said, wiping his mouth on the paper napkin before he slid out of the booth and made his way to the back.

Sam couldn't help it; she watched his very fine butt until he disappeared down the hallway. With the final swallow of coffee, she pulled bills out of a pocket and slipped them under the bill. After a moment of remembrance for her aching feet while waitressing in college, she added another bill. However, when she reached for her backpack and the messenger bag, she recognized the flaw in her idea. Christopher's backpack sat on the bench opposite her.

If she took it with her, someone would notice. If people noticed, they remembered. If she left it behind, he would have no change of clothes. She couldn't stop the grin, enjoying the image of the man walking naked around whatever room they booked. Of course, if last night was anything to go by, it hardly mattered if he had his backpack of belongings or not.

"Ready?"

Caught day-dreaming, she looked up as Christopher reached for his backpack with one hand, extended the other to her. Her first instinct was annoyance that he hadn't followed her instructions. Then, she had to give him credit for coming to the same conclusion about the backpack as she had. And he'd come up with a solution. She reached for him and they walked out to the car. They drove aimlessly for hours.

When she spotted the combination hardware and farm supply store shortly after noon, she pulled into the parking lot. Two trucks, an SUV and a small sedan were parked closest to the door. Enough people to hopefully keep him from being recognized.

"Go inside," she told Christopher, shifting in the seat to look at him. It was a risk, one she felt was necessary. Hopefully, between the cap, the two-day beard and if he said very little, he'd be able to pull this off. She drew bills from their dwindling stack out of her pocket, handed them over.

"Get a pair of scissors. Any kind, it doesn't matter."

His gaze roamed over her hair. "Are you sure?"

"I told you I'll do whatever's necessary."

His hand closed over the money, held her hand. "I'll be careful." He leaned over, kissed her and left the car.

She watched him, her heart climbing in her throat, pounding with each second he was out of her sight. If she'd made a mistake by letting him go inside instead of her, she'd never forgive herself. Another time she'd hesitated to take action had nearly resulted in the loss of a life. She gripped the steering wheel and promised she wouldn't let it happen again.

A gust of breath shot out of her when he walked out and returned to the car, a paper bag in his hand. She said nothing, simply waited for him to buckle his seat belt and put the car in reverse. They continued to drive in silence until she spotted a sign for a rest area. By-passing the restrooms, she drove around to the cluster of picnic tables, thankfully all empty.

"Let's get this done," she said and got out.

"Do you want me to do it?" Christopher asked.

"I've got it." He took the scissors out of the bag and handed them over. Not giving herself time to think, Sam grabbed hold of the ponytail and cut it off in two thick scissoring cuts, just above the band. A warm breeze on her exposed neck had a shiver skating down her spine. She handed the hank of hair to him, and continued trimming it as best she could without a mirror.

"Let me," he said, easing the scissors out of her grip. With a gentleness that nearly undid her, he snipped and used his fingertips to fluff and arrange the strands. He stepped in front of her, used the tips of the scissors to fashion bangs. With a small smile, he looked into her eyes.

"They're a little ragged, but I remember once, only once, my mom tried to trim my sister's bangs. The more she tried to even them out, the shorter they become."

She grabbed the scissors from him. "I'm sure it's fine."

"Samantha." He framed her face with his hands, his smile gone. He softly brushed his lips over hers. "You look lovely."

"Maybe I should have cut it sooner. I've always heard long hair makes a woman look older. At least we'll blend in together a little better now." She stepped out his hold when his eyes flashed with anger, gestured to the hair on the table. "Toss that in the trash, will you. Then, let's move on."

"I KNOW we were out of the car at the rest stop, but would it be possible for us to stop and stretch our legs a little?" Christopher asked, when they approached a small town.

She started to say no, made herself pause. It had been more than an hour, a silent hour, since they'd left the rest stop. Throughout this escape, he hadn't complained or argued any decision she'd made. And she'd caught him shifting on the seat, trying to get more comfortable for the last hour. She parked in a spot in front of a bookstore that also housed a coffee shop. After some discussion they decided to risk stowing the backpacks in the trunk rather than carry them. She slipped the messenger bag over her shoulder as she scanned the street.

The street was clean, the windows of the various businesses all sported signs of holiday sales in addition to colorful decorations. She spotted an antique shop, what appeared to be a Bed and Breakfast, a travel agency, and an old-fashioned drug store, complete with a soda fountain counter.

"Now we're talking."

Christopher grabbed her hand and jay-walked her across the street. Obviously in a better mood, he grinned up at the marque of a movie theatre that had undoubtably been built back in the forties. Today's double feature were the holiday classics *Miracle on 42nd Street* and *It's a Wonderful Life.*

"I thought you wanted to stretch your legs."

"C'mon, Sam. What better place to hide than at a movie?" He gestured to the theatre. "We'll eat popcorn." He wiggled his brows. "And sit in the last row where we can neck like we did in high school."

"I never necked in high school."

"Never?" he asked, his face conveying disbelief.

"No. As I've tried to explain, I didn't have the kind of upbringing you did."

He threw an arm around her shoulders. She could feel the warmth and strength of his muscles against her exposed neck. "Then I'll have the pleasure of showing you how it's done."

He did a damn fine job of it. In between those hot kisses it was nice to snuggle close with his arm around her. They ate a gallon of popcorn, heavy on the salt and butter at her insistence, while watching innocence and holiday hope play out on screen in black and white.

Then, they walked outside to see the local police - young, possibly a rookie she decided - noting down the license plate number of their car.

"Should we walk away?" Christopher asked.

"No." She stepped off the curb and made her way to the car. "Problem, officer?"

He looked over, shifted, brought his left hand

up to rest on his hip. Within reach of his gun. "You've been parked here for more than four hours."

"Yes." She smiled. "We took in the double feature."

The office gestured to the license plate with the notepad he held, indicating he'd run the tag. "You came all this way from LA to see a movie?"

It took no effort to put some sultry promise in her voice when she looked at Christopher. "We wanted to get away."

"It was my idea." He wrapped an arm around her waist, tugged her close so he could press a kiss to her temple. "This is a hard time for Pepper since she lost her husband about this time last year. I wanted to try and cheer her up. You know, give her a good memory to replace the bad."

"He had a heart attack." She sniffed. "I know people thought I only married Jock for his money, but I loved him."

"Of course, you did, baby." He kissed her temple again and looked back at the cop, who had a bemused look on his face. "Our next stop is Ontario and Logan's Candy Shop." He smiled. "It just seemed the right place to go."

"Well." The officer stepped back, giving them

room to go to their car doors. Christopher stayed in character by following Sam and opening her door when she clicked the remote to unlock it. "You have a safe trip." He touched the brim of his hat. "And I'm sorry about your husband, ma'am."

"Thank you."

While she buckled her seat belt and started the engine, Christopher settled in his seat. The officer continued to watch as they pulled out the space and started down the street.

"Pepper?" Sam asked.

"Sweetheart, I told you I think you're hot."

With a snort of laughter, she headed east.

CHAPTER 7

IN A CHEERFUL MOOD, nothing like two good flicks, about the holidays no less, to help a man forget his troubles. Add in a sexy woman whose kisses had Christopher thinking of all the wild and wicked ways he wanted to be with her – and knowing she was open to all those possibilities - and he figured life just didn't get much better.

Until he recalled the reason for the afternoon escape, and why that woman was with him here and now, was because he'd been accused of theft and murder.

He'd gone stone cold when they left the theatre and spotted the cop, when Sam marched right over and confronted him. He should have known she had a plan. She would do whatever it took to keep him, them, safe.

He could picture her doing much the same when she left the Secret Service and moved to Montana. As she used the crutch of alcohol to chase away the sense of failure, loneliness and heartache. And as she battled back to stand on her own.

Small wonder he was crazy about her.

He'd never given much thought to being with a woman long-term. He'd been so focused on his career. Being selfish, some, including members of his family, called him. He wasn't ashamed to admit he liked being the sole focus of Sam's attention. He liked even more knowing he gave her the kind of affection and appreciation she'd had far too little of in her life.

When this was all over, he thought they'd both enjoying spending some time at her place in Montana. They'd ride her horses, share some wine and make love in front of a roaring fire. He was enough of a California boy to want to play in the snow. For a short time anyway.

"What kind of dog?"

"Sorry? What?" she asked, looking at him.

"You said you were thinking of getting a dog. What kind."

"Oh." She went back to watching the road. "I don't know. Something small, I think. You know, so it can keep my lap warm in the evenings when I'm reading."

"Nope," he cheerfully disagreed. "Something small won't work. Not for you."

"Is that so?"

"You need the kind of dog that lays at your feet, one who would stand between you and trouble."

"No one stands between me and trouble."

"See there, a small dog'd be bad for your reputation. And," he trailed off as she failed to keep her lips from curving. "You were jerking my chain."

Her laughter rolled out, carefree and joyful. He felt pride swell inside him, knowing he was responsible for making her happy. Need rose in him, sudden and fierce, a need that only she could quiet. He released his seat belt.

"Christopher? What are you doing?"

"Find a back road, Sam." He tugged down the zipper on his jeans, arched his hips and shimmed his jeans down to his ankles. He hissed out a breath as his erection, hard as stone, jutted out.

"Chris." He noted that though she protested, she slowed the car, was looking around.

"Don't stop here for God's sake. Someone might come along and think we need help. What I need is your hands on me," he said, stroking his own up and down his shaft. She glanced his way and he saw all he needed to see. His urgency had ignited hers. "Now." Sweat broke out on his skin and he gritted his teeth when she took the turn-off fast enough to have the car protesting on the dirt road.

The instant she braked to a stop in a bare spot behind a cluster of bushes, he reached over and cut the engine. With a release of her seat belt she was on him, her mouth taking his in a kiss that had him hoping, praying, he could maintain control. Then, that hot, giving mouth left his. And took him in. His long appreciative moan reverberated throughout the car.

She took him to the edge. Several times. Just when he thought he couldn't hold on, when he feared he'd short-change them both, she slowed, dialed back the frenzied need. Only to have it rising again. Finally, he cupped his hands under her arms, brought her back to his mouth.

Between laughter, grunts, moans and

complaints about the lack of room, they managed to get her pants off. He speared a finger in her, then two. His thumb found the sensual nub, rubbed it. And he watched with dazed delight as she reared back, her eyes closed, and exploded around him. Her release, and his pleasure at giving it to her, should have lessened the need. Instead it had the desire for her pounding harder, stronger.

She maneuvered over to straddle him, to sink down on him, to hold him in that most intimate way a woman could hold a man. And he found everything he wanted in life.

And he wanted it forever.

No wonder he'd had this need rise up in him so strong and sure. It shook him, this unexpected revelation that he loved her. And it saddened him, because he knew she wasn't ready to accept his declaration.

Wasn't ready to believe in the honesty of his love.

So, instead of voicing the words in his heart, he let her ride him, let her take what he'd started and use him to give her the release her body demanded, and offered, both of them.

"What the hell?" Her breath panted hot at his neck. "Was that?"

"Baby, if you don't know I'll have to take you through it again." His hands roamed under the shirt he'd not taken off her, slid up her back to flick open the clasp of her bra.

"You can't be serious." She levered back enough to look into his face. He was already hard again. "Oh, my God, you are."

"Hmm." He sampled her taste just under her chin. "I could do more if we move to the backseat."

"Maybe you could, but I can't." She looked around, adorably confused by the situation and the way they were tangled together.

"I still can't believe I did this. Plus, it was irresponsible." Sam paused, shook her head. "I'm on the pill, it's not that you didn't put on a condom."

"You mean, when you didn't give me time to put one on."

Her cheeks went pink. "What if someone had come by and seen us? This can't happen again."

He framed her face, loving how his hands could comb through her short hair now. It humbled him to realize she'd done that for him, as a measure of protection for him. Thankful for her, loving her, he guided her down so he could kiss her long and hard. Contrary to her words, her inner muscles contracted around him in response. He didn't see them making it onto that back seat.

"Let me prove you wrong."

STAGGERED BY HER BEHAVIOR, Sam settled behind the steering wheel. She might ignore the self-satisfied smirk on Christopher's face, but she knew damn well she had one of her own circling in her thoughts. Her heart had yet to relax into a normal rhythm.

She'd had sex – twice – within the confines of a small sedan behind bushes on the side of the road. Never in her life would she have believed herself capable of the kind of gymnastics that had been required to do what they'd done to each other on the front seat of the car.

It had been a mistake, a dangerous risk, to indulge the outrageous passion he'd aroused in her. She could hardly protect him with her pants, gun, and a fortune in diamonds, around her ankles while she rode his cock hard and fast.

Given the opportunity, she'd do it again.

And that thought reminded her that they were running out of time and options.

"We need to do something."

"Sam." He sighed. "I love the way you're think-ing, but seriously, I'm going to need a little recovery time."

She might have laughed, at least have smiled, only the seriousness of their situation suddenly slammed into her with new intensity. Was it because they'd become lovers that she now felt even more responsibility for ensuring his safety? Even before this journey, she'd admitted he wasn't a shallow actor concerned with his own image.

He was kind and sensitive. He had a quirky sense of humor and a child-like enjoyment of life. He could kiss and touch her like no one ever had.

She was deathly afraid he'd gotten to close to the heart she'd kept barred and protected for most of her life.

"We can't keep riding around, avoiding people," she said, more comfortable with focusing on coming up with a plan rather than confront her emotions.

He skimmed a fingertip down her cheek, then over to flip at the shortened ends of her hair before he lightly settled his hand on her shoulder. "What do you have in mind?"

"I'm not sure. I'd feel better if we heard from

Hank. And no," she said, giving him a quick look. "I don't think we should contact him."

"I trust you." With them entering town, he dropped a little lower in his seat. "Let me know when you've decided."

She studied the streets as she rifled through various scenarios for a plan. Then, as they stopped at a traffic light, a building a little further down on a corner caught her eye.

"The library?" Christopher asked as she parked and cut the engine.

"Research. We can use one of the public computers and look at news sources to see if there's anything we need to know about the investigation into Tyler's murder." She patted the bag slung over her shoulder. "We can look for where these came from." They got out and she looked at him over the roof of the car. "It's not much of a plan."

"It's a start."

They backtracked to the day of the murder, read everything they could find. They were no more informed than when they entered the library. However, to Sam's astonishment, Christopher proved to have fluid and talented computer skills. Bouncing from one news item to another, digging deeper and in places she would have never considered, he uncovered a series of reports on the thefts of several small quantities of diamonds from pawn shops located in and around downtown Los Angeles.

Apparently, the thefts had been random and separated enough by both time and location the police had not connected them. And while the reports hadn't listed the size or number of diamonds missing from each location, her instinct told her they'd found the source of the diamonds hanging around her shoulder.

Diamonds that had already caused the death of one young man.

"How did you do that?" Sam asked.

He grinned while wiggling his fingers. "I have many talents," he said in a low, thick Russian accent.

"As much as I appreciate your skill in uncovering this information, it doesn't help us know what to do next."

"Maybe a walk will free up ideas."

"Walk?"

"Sure." He closed out the links he'd used, took her hand and stood. "It's something I do whenever I need to figure out the best approach to a scene or character. If you let your mind roam, you'd be surprised by what little revelations can come your way."

Sam let Christopher talk her into taking the time, into walking the streets along with all the other tourists. Her mind, however, wasn't as relaxed as he'd predicted.

It didn't feel right to her. She was accustomed to doing something, not strolling down the street taking in all the Christmas decorations, trying not to stare at the people who passed by. Ignoring the tingle of nerves tap-dancing along her spine. She was used to searching the surroundings for threats, watching for suspicious movements or behavior, her every muscle tensed and primed for action.

There had to be a way to lure Jerry into a confrontation, a confession. Somewhere along the way she must have overlooked a vital clue. If she could only have some quiet time to think back, to go over the details, she was sure she could come up with the perfect solution.

She wanted to be the one controlling the action, not reacting to it.

"Relax," Christopher said, slinging an arm

around her shoulder, grinning at her. "Enjoy the moment."

"We should be doing something."

"We are." He leaned over to skim her mouth with his. "We're spending time together."

And, no matter what happened next, that time was rapidly fading. So, with a concentrated effort, she willed her muscles to relax.

He took such joy in whatever he did. He laughed at the antics of the performers on the town square, pointed out with enthusiasm the unique as well as the traditional decorations, his face glowed in the colorful reflection of the lights.

At Logan's Candies, they watched the candy cane making demonstration, then paid the small fee to mold their own. Her imagination reached only far enough to go with a simple S design.

Christopher grinned with delighted satisfaction as he showed off his diamond shaped design. "It just seemed right."

Was it any wonder she'd fallen in love with him?

She stumbled back a step at the stunning admission. Doing so saved their lives.

A speeding car come closer seconds before she

heard the screams. The stupid driver ignored innocent bystanders, including children, as he jumped the curb and steered the car onto the sidewalk. Not hesitating, she grabbed a fistful of Christopher's shirt and shoved him into the crowd running out of range of the approaching car. She turned to hurry after him, but not fast enough to avoid having her ass kissed by the brush of the car as it drove by.

"Damn it," she swore, her knees and palms sliding and scraping on the sidewalk.

"Sam." He crouched beside her, clutched her against his chest. "What the hell were you thinking?"

"Protecting you." She swore again, rose to her feet, surveyed the crowd. People were crying, holding onto one another, tending to injuries. Thankfully they appeared mostly surface knocks and scrapes. A few were interested only in posting video of the aftermath on social media. Sirens told her cops were fast approaching. "C'mon, we need to get out of here."

"We can't just leave. These people need help."

"Not ours. We have to get as far away as possible before the cops get here."

"Wait." He tugged her hand, pointed in the opposite direction. "The car this's way."

"They knew we were here. We can't go back." The car that rammed the crowd wouldn't be there waiting for them. It was long gone, heading away from town. But there would be another one waiting, oh yeah, they'd tag team, believing Sam and Christopher's first instinct would be to get to the car and escape.

"It's how they tracked us. The cop outside the theatre ran our plates. You said the property manager has friends with the police. They must have alerted him when that cop ran our tags and he sent someone to find us."

While they'd been playing tourist. While she'd faced the fact that she'd fallen in love.

Christopher stopped, stared at her, his eyes blazing with fury. "There were children in the crowd."

"I know." Ignoring the sick roll of her stomach, she looked around, searching for the best place to hide in plain sight.

It became a moot point when Christopher grabbed her arm, swung her around and pinned her to the wall. He stepped between her legs, giving the impression they were a couple sharing gratitude for not being hurt. At some point he'd lost the cap she'd bought him. With everything they'd faced in the past five minutes, it seemed shallow to miss seeing him wearing it.

"This ends now," he ground out. "Give me the phone. He can have the damned diamonds."

She looped her arms around his neck, furthering the image of bound lovers while keeping him from storming away. "It's more than the diamonds," she said, leaning forward to whisper in his ear. "You've been accused of murder."

His body jerked against hers, his heart pounding in perfect tandem with hers as the rising tide of his distress washed over her. She figured he'd somehow forgotten that aspect of why they'd been on the run. Had gotten lost somewhere between the first frantic dash off the studio lot and tonight's close escape from a deadly driver.

With a whole lot of damned good sex thrown in between.

"We've got to do something, Sam." Christopher lifted his head, glanced back to the noise of the scene they'd left behind.

"I couldn't live with myself if someone died because I ran."

She started to argue that he could, that she had for most of her life. But, because she did understand the sentiment, she knew she'd do whatever it took to save him from a life of regret and nightmares.

She brushed brush back his hair before she lightly pressed her mouth to his.

"Let's find somewhere we can sit, maybe have some coffee." She swept over his lips once more. "And come up with a plan."

CHAPTER 8

THEY WENT TO A BAR INSTEAD. Hideaway was the type of place where you went when you wanted to drink unnoticed. Or if you were meeting unsavory business associates or an illicit lover.

Sam quietly ordered and paid for two bottled beers before she and Christopher settled in a dark corner booth. A part of her wanted to cuddle him close and stroke away the images burning in his gaze. But that would help only in the short term. They needed to look at the big picture. The turn of phrase clicked something inside her.

"The movie," she said. "Remember when I suggested rewriting some of the pivotal scenes to show your character getting Sadie's to open up, trust him with running an op to stop the bastards blackmailing her into committing the heists?"

"Yes," he said. "She had to act like bait to flush out the masterminds, promise to cooperate with him fully. Is that..."

"The only way we can catch Jerry is to trap him. But there's a risk." She took a drink of her beer, hoping the cold taste would slide past the way her throat wanted to close. "You could end up taking the fall for the theft. Or worse, get killed in the crossfire."

"How would it work?"

It humbled her that he didn't hesitate. That he trusted her. So, she did something she'd done with very few people in her life. She trusted in return.

Over the first beer, she outlined the rough plan. Over the second beer, and some questionable nachos, they debated, considered, altered. Knowing they took a chance at being located, they made two short phone calls, asking for information and assistance.

With the burner phone on the table between them, they stared at one another. "Are you sure?" Sam asked.

Christopher looked to the door of the bar.

Twice people had come inside talking about the accident. Even the police had stepped inside for one tense minute, taken a look around, then backed out. As far as Sam could see, the biggest flaw in the plan was making the first contact here, where they could be overheard. On the other hand, the only person who'd paid them the slightest attention was the worn-out waitress who'd delivered their beer and nachos.

"All I have to do is remember that scene outside." He picked up the phone, punched in the number they'd asked Sadie to give them, and held the phone so Sam could overhear the conversation.

"Jerry," he said when the call was answered with a terse hello. "You went too far."

"You've got my diamonds."

Sam put her hand on Christopher's thigh, squeezed once. He nodded his understanding. The idea was for him to sound remorseful, play to Jerry's need to hold something over him. "I didn't know I had them when I ran away. God, Jerry, that guy killed Tyler. I wasn't going to go anywhere with him."

"You've got my diamonds," he repeated as if they hadn't just been discussing murder.

"That's right." He paused, heard the faint clicking. "Don't bother tracing the call, you won't find out where I am until I'm ready for you to know."

"You sound cocky, Chris." The clicking continued. "That's not like you."

"Not cocky." He lifted his head, studied the room. Sam could feel the anger vibrating inside him, the loss of respect for someone he'd once considered a likable co-worker. But he had a role to play.

"What I am, is desperate. I've got a career, Jerry. At least I had one. I want it back. Just think, if we figure this out we can work together in the future." He paused. "I don't have any vices like Tyler." He forced out a chuckle, making it sound shaky with nerves. "Well, okay I do enjoy the women my career gives me. But, Jerry, they won't interfere with our arrangement. You think about it," he finished and cut the call.

This time Sam didn't resist the urge to cuddle, although she only hugged him with a single arm around his shoulders.

"Why don't we get out of here?"

He nodded, stood and offered a hand. "Where are we going anyway?"

She smiled, and tripped over her own feet. It

was a risk to focus attention on them, but she had a purpose in mind. With a laugh, she looped her arms around Christopher's neck. He looked at her, puzzled but she kissed him to prevent him from saying anything. "Hmm, you're tasty, lover."

When she pulled away and took his hand to lead him out, she bumped into the table of a man she'd spotted earlier. He was early thirties, had the look of a man hoping to drown his sorrows – and had spent the last hour doing just that.

Her bump not only spilled his freshly delivered beer, it tipped his wallet onto the floor. "I'm sorry. I'm sorry." Sam squatted down, scooped up the wallet, where it had flipped open to reveal a photo. "Oh, is this your wife?"

"Girlfriend," the man muttered. "At least she was. Wants to be my wife?"

Using a confused expression, Sam looked at him. "You don't love her?"

"I do. I love her more than I thought possible." He swept a hand over his face, took a deep breath, the kind a diver takes before plunging into deep water. "She wants to get married. But what if I mess it up?"

"What if you don't?" Sam folded the wallet,

handed it back to him. He looked her in the eye. "Love should make you afraid of making mistakes. It should also give you the courage to try." She took his hand, had him standing with her. "Go to her. Talk to her."

"You think she'll listen?"

"I do." She turned him. "Go on, I'll cover your tab. Good luck," she said, giving him a push. She drew bills out of her pocket, and, as if drinking had made it difficult for her, took a careful count of them before she placed several on the table

"You didn't have too much to drink," Christopher said once they were in the parking lot.

"Nope, and I feel really bad about taking advantage of a man who looked about as unhappy as a man could be. But." She held up the credit card she'd slipped out with. "He should be more careful about leaving his wallet on the table."

With the town packed with tourists, it took awhile to find a room. It was more expensive than Sam felt comfortable charging on a stolen card, but mentally promised she'd send payment to the guy once they were out of this. Provided their plan worked.

In the room, they took turns showering. Sam

washed out her underwear, hung it over the shower bar and, wrapped in a towel, left the bathroom. It didn't surprise her to find Christopher on the bed, naked beneath the sheet he'd pulled up to his waist, his eyes closed, his chest rising and falling in a steady rhythm. Her heart filled with love, and more fear than she could admit, as she dropped the towel and snuggled up against him. He murmured. But he wrapped an arm around her to hold her close.

And she learned he wasn't asleep as she'd believed.

"I need you," he whispered, stroking a hand down her hip, back up to cup her breast. He was slow, deliberate. Her pulse scrambled.

She knew he was using her as an outlet for all the tension and turmoil of the past few hours. So, he could forget, for a few moments, the images of people, children, huddled on the street, frightened and hurt. Because of him.

She felt the same.

Turning, she sighed as the warmth chased away her chills, as his touch ignited a fire inside her, as his kisses had her mind spinning and filling with soft, lovely images. They moved together, caressing, offering, with a tenderness that had tears burning behind her closed lids.

He cared for her, she felt it in every touch as he urged to one peak, followed quickly by another. Because it was more than she'd ever known, she accepted freely. When she felt him tremble, she stroked, not to soothe but to excite. When she rolled over and slid down to take him inside, she took them both on the fast, urgent ride to escape all they didn't want to face.

And what she couldn't say.

IN THE MORNING, grateful for the room amenities, Sam nursed a cup of in-room coffee while using the complimentary hair dryer to dry her underwear.

"You could go commando."

She glanced in the sink mirror and saw the reflection of Christopher's devilish smile. Since his briefs hung next to her panties, she knew that was the choice he'd made. She really hoped that distracting thought didn't come back to her at a crucial point today.

Within an hour, after again wiping down all

surfaces, they walked outside into the bright sunshine. The lights for all the Christmas decorations were off but it seemed to her that the air carried the faint scent of pine and sugar cookies. In spite of what happened last night, the town, to her way of thinking, also spoke of the innocent faith and hope of the season.

"Are you sure?" she asked Christopher as they settled on a bench with to-go coffee. "There's still time to come up with another plan."

He turned to her, in that way he had, the way that always made her heart skip, and framed her face with his hands. "The one honest thing I told Jerry yesterday is I want my career back." He kissed her lightly. "I want my life back." He kissed her, a little longer this time. "I want a weekend with you, alone at a decadent hotel where we can spend time together without worry."

She smiled because she thought it would ease his mind. "You want a weekend of sex." Her smile came easier when he laughed.

"Got me."

No, I don't. At least not for much longer.

They finished their coffee and started walking to their destination. Since they took back streets, stopping occasionally as if they were interested in some holiday display or another, it took them longer to arrive at the agreed-upon spot than she'd anticipated. Long enough that Jerry, along with another man, sat on a bench beneath a tree, waiting for them. The man sitting beside him used a knife to sharpen a branch into a deadly point. It had a sizzle of nerves doing cartwheels in her stomach.

"That's the one," Christopher whispered. "The one who stabbed Tyler."

Around them, monuments and markers showed tribute to death. While the atmosphere was serene, she didn't let down her guard.

"Where are my diamonds?" Jerry demanded. The man beside him didn't look their way.

"Right here." Christopher patted the strap of the messenger bag resting at his hip.

At the sound of an approaching car on the gravel lane, they stood quiet. Two rows over the car stopped. A man and woman, backs bowed with grief and the woman holding a bouquet of flowers, knelt in front of a grave marker.

"I have to admit I never would have pegged you for this, Jerry."

He grinned. "That's why it's been so easy to get away with."

"Do you steal the jewels from the pawn shops?" Sam asked. "Or are you just involved with holding them until they're cold?"

"Got yourself a smart girl here, Christopher." Jerry ran a hand over his thinning hair. "I'm what you could call middle management."

"How long have you been doing this?" Christopher asked.

"Long enough to have known better than to have trusted Tyler. The kid was a screw up from the get-go. If we hadn't gotten to him, someone else would have."

"So, you did him a favor by having your associate here knife him before someone else could." He shook his head. "I don't understand you, Jerry."

"We did what had to be done. I've got people on my back," Jerry said. "Give me the diamonds and I promise I'll find a way to clear your name so you can your career back."

"I could do that." He winked at Sam. "But we have a better idea." He lifted a hand, gave a quick wave. The man walked toward them, leaning on a cane. "Tyler, be careful, the ground's uneven."

"No way," Jerry said, jumping to his feet,

looking at the man beside him. "I saw you stab him."

"I did."

"You did," Christopher confirmed. "But obviously you were more interested in chasing after me than you were in making sure Tyler didn't recover." Christopher grinned. "Now that he has, he can free my name."

"While you and your associate here," Sam said. "Go to prison for theft, murder, and accessory after the fact." She lifted her cell phone, tilted it. "I've recorded this entire conversation, that would be your confessions, so the cops will believe Christopher's story. And yes," she continued. "I know you believe you have plenty of cops to protect you. But, what about the people you work for? How long do you think they're going to let you live and turn on them? That's what happens when you make dangerous business arrangements." She whipped the gun out and stepped in front of Christopher when the man made a lunge toward them, his knife point threatening. "You're going to want to put that away."

She heard Christopher swear at the way she stood in front of him. Didn't care. She'd do whatever it took to protect him. Thankfully, the man with the knife could see that in her gaze. He dropped the knife to the ground.

The grieving man and woman stood, walked their way. The man held a gun while keeping the woman a step behind him. "We'll take it from here, Sam."

"Let me at least have the pleasure of introducing you first," she said, returning her gaze to Jerry. "This is Duke Morris and his wife, Angel. Duke is former military and works with the Brotherhood Protectors." The sound of approaching sirens echoed in the silence. "That would be the authorities Duke alerted. Oh, and since you obviously didn't recognize him, over there." She pointed her gun toward the man with the cane, who slipped the wig off his head. "That's Randy. He was Tyler's stunt double."

When the police arrived, it took all of two seconds for Jerry and his accomplice to start scrambling to implicate each other and make a deal. It didn't bother her that it felt slightly anticlimactic. All that mattered was Christopher was safe and could return to the career he loved. And, it didn't hurt her feelings any to have the authorities take the bag of diamonds into their possession.

The police separated them for questioning and

a detailing of their activities since the day of Tyler's murder. They'd even been kept apart when they were driven back to Los Angeles, where they again had to separately go over all the details. She'd expected that. What she hadn't expected was the hole it carved inside her to be without him. When she was finally released, she'd been told that Christopher, released hours earlier, had been picked up by his parents. Resigned, knowing it was for the best, she went to the room at a long-stay hotel the Brotherhood Protectors had rented for her to use while consulting for the movie. She refused to cry, but it was a close call when, well after midnight as she channel-surfed and no doubt spurred by recent events, she came across Christopher's first movie.

For the next two days she ran errands, reassured Sadie, who'd returned to Montana for Christmas, that she was fine, spoke with Hank, and even had a lunch meeting with the movie director to go over a few details for filming the new sequences she'd suggested. She finally managed several hours of uninterrupted sleep before the landline rang.

"Is this Samantha Ethridge?" came a crisp, straightforward voice.

"Yes, who is this?"

"Roberta Ethridge. Christopher's mother."

"Uh." She swept a hand through her hair, startled a little more awake at the new reality of her short hair.

The voice softened now, almost to a whisper. "I wanted to thank you for keeping my boy safe. I know he's a grown man, but he's still my boy. He's told me all about you so I wanted to make sure you have our address."

"Address?"

"Yes, so you can come for Christmas." She rattled off the address. "Come anytime. The kids will have us up before dawn." Before she could protest or come up with any excuse, the phone went dead.

"Well, hell. What am I supposed to do now?"

Two hours later, she stood on the doorstep of a sprawling ranch-style house. A wreath hung on the door and lights were strung along the eaves. She had a trembling hand outstretched to ring the bell when it suddenly opened.

"You're here." Christopher pulled her into a tight embrace that had the package in her arms digging into her stomach. His cheek, clean shaven once again, pressed against hers, his arms held her close. "God, I've missed you."

Then, oh then, he eased back enough to lift his hands to cup her face. He kissed her, a soft kiss that had her knees trembling along with her hands. How the hell was she supposed to say good-bye and forget him when he filled her so completely?

"Excuse me," she managed with a forced smile when he drew away. "What's your name?"

He threw back his head and laughed. "Merry Christmas, Sam." He gave her a quick kiss. "And welcome to bedlam."

The description wasn't far off. Wrapping paper and discarded packages littered the floor, along with children playing with electronic hand-held games, stacking blocks or playing with dolls. Scents of coffee and something sweet filled the air.

She was hugged, thanked, introduced to far more people than she'd ever remember names for, and was made to feel welcomed.

"I brought cookies," Sam said, offering the box to his mother after the woman had wrapped her in a snug embrace, along with a whispered, "Thank you for coming."

The plastic window on the box showed red and

white stripped candy cane shaped cookies. She looked at Christopher. "They seemed appropriate."

"More than you know," he said.

It was several hours later before she was able to make her excuses and say good-bye. She and Christopher walked to her rental car with the sky gone rosy red with approaching darkness.

"I got you a Christmas present."

"Yeah?"

She laughed a little, pulled the wrapped box out of the car. Leaning against the closed door, she laughed again at the way he made quick work of the brightly colored paper. His eyes were as bright as the reflecting colored lights around his home as he lifted out the ball cap.

"You did say you were an Angels fan."

He slipped it on, grinned at her. "I have a present for you also." Her palms tingled as he placed the small jeweler's box he drew out of his pocket into her hands. Fear, along with a hope she didn't dare acknowledge, had her staring, unable to move.

He finally stripped off the paper, let it fall to the ground to join his and flipped open the lid. Nestled within the white satin was a band of alternating rubies and diamonds.

"I wanted something to remind us both of making candy canes. I love you, Sam." He reached for her numb hand, slipped on the band before she could protest. "Marry me." He closed his mouth over hers.

Her heart soared and it took every fiber within her to resist binding him to her. Because she did love him, more than she believed possible, she knew she couldn't.

When his mouth lifted, she used a hand to press against his chest. It was her damn bad luck, it was her left hand. She shook her head, closing her eyes for a minute to gather her resolve.

"Christopher, what you're feeling is misplaced affection. We went through a stressful situation, had only each other to depend on. It's only natural ---"

"That's bullshit and you know it." He wrapped a hand around her chin, lifted her face so she had no choice but to look at him. "Tell me you don't love me."

"I can't." She shook her head, twisting but not removing the beautiful band from her finger. "It's because I love you that I have to tell you no. I told myself the age difference between us doesn't matter."

"It doesn't."

"Damn it, Chris." She shoved at his chest. He didn't budge. "You live and work in Hollywood. You know damn well age matters. Women are looked at as old as they age, while men are considered distinguished and in their prime."

"It doesn't matter." He reached for her hand, pressed it to his heart where she could feel the steady beat of his heart. "In here it doesn't matter."

"I can't give you children, Christopher."

"I don't want them."

She looked at the house, at the brightly colored lights, the knowledge of the warmth, friendship and love that filled the interior. "I might have believed that before I saw you with your family."

"It's because of my family I don't want my own. Yes, they're happy that I'm safe. Because of you," he said, lifting her hand to brush his lips over the ring. "I love them, enjoy them. But, the kind of life they have doesn't fit me. Hell, half of them are probably staring out the window at us now."

She managed to not look to the house, instead kept her gaze locked on his.

"It's more than just acting that makes me different from them," he said. "I want to travel. I want you to be free to go with me, whether it's for a movie or because there's somewhere we want to explore. Call me selfish, but I like the idea of not sharing you with anyone, of knowing I'm free to give you all the love and attention you've never had."

"What if you change your mind?"

He smiled and her heart trembled on the brink of surrender. "What if I don't? Isn't that what you told the guy in the bar? Love should give you the courage to try." He leaned forward, kissed her. "Try with me, Samantha. I promise I'll never want to escape."

"We could just live together."

He was already shaking his head no before she finished the suggestion. "I don't ever want you to think I'm not committed to you. To us." He kissed her again. "I love you, Samantha. Marry me. Make a life with me. Share your life with me." He pressed her hand to his heart. "Be my life."

How could she fight his belief? His love? Especially when her heart yearned to have everything he promised. She heard sincerity in his voice, saw the depth of his love in his blue eyes. She knew her love for him filled all the empty places inside her.

"Just in case you ever think of dumping me, you

might want to stop and consider the fact that I know all kinds of ways to hurt you."

His smile was like the sun coming back out, raining warmth and pleasure over them. "I'm not worried."

She framed his face in her hands. "Then I won't be either."

https://amzn.to/2GB8Hh4

UNCOVER RESCUE

https://amzn.to/2CTNQpq

THE RANCHER'S REPLACEMENT WIFE

https://amzn.to/2KZudhK

BAREFOOT BAY

HOT SUMMER KISSES

https://bit.ly/2xnH2u4

THE PILOT'S PROMISE

https://bit.ly/2D58zGv

WILD ROSE PRESS

COURTING THE COACH

http://amzn.to/2k88Xu6

SHARED SECRETS

http://amzn.to/29reioM

CRYSTAL CLEAR

http://amzn.to/2kNsYW9

BROTHERHOOD PROTECTORS

ORIGINAL SERIES BY ELLE JAMES

Brotherhood Protectors Series

Montana SEAL (#1)

Bride Protector SEAL (#2)

Montana D-Force (#3)

Cowboy D-Force (#4)

Montana Ranger (#5)

Montana Dog Soldier (#6)

Montana SEAL Daddy (#7)

Montana Ranger's Wedding Vow (#8)

Montana SEAL Undercover Daddy (#9)

Cape Cod SEAL Rescue (#10)

Montana SEAL Friendly Fire (#11)

Montana SEAL's Mail-Order Bride (#12)

SEAL Justice (#13)

Ranger Creed (#14)

Delta Force Rescue (#15)

Montana Rescue (Sleeper SEAL)

Hot SEAL Salty Dog (SEALs in Paradise)

ABOUT ELLE JAMES

ELLE JAMES also writing as MYLA JACKSON is a *New York Times* and *USA Today* Bestselling author of books including cowboys, intrigues and paranormal adventures that keep her readers on the edges of their seats. With over eighty works in a variety of sub-genres and lengths she has published with Harlequin, Samhain, Ellora's Cave, Kensington, Cleis Press, and Avon. When she's not at her computer, she's traveling, snow skiing, boating, or riding her ATV, dreaming up new stories. Learn more about Elle James at www.elle-james.com

Website | Facebook | Twitter | GoodReads | Newsletter | BookBub | Amazon

Follow Elle!
www.ellejames.com
ellejames@ellejames.com

Made in the USA
Columbia, SC
22 December 2020